EVERY GOOD GIFT

A CHRISTIAN SUSPENSE NOVEL

URCELIA TEIXEIRA

EVERY GOOD GIFT

AN ADAM CROSS CHRISTIAN SUSPENSE

URCELIA TEIXEIRA

Copyrighted material
EBook © ISBN: 978-0-6398434-4-5
Paperback © ISBN: 978-0-6398434-5-2
Independently Published by Urcelia Teixeira
First edition
Urcelia Teixeira
Wiltshire, UK

www.urcelia.com
books@urcelia.com

To Chanel, my dearest friend and sister in Christ
Your obedience to God led to my
spiritual re-awakening, which in turn, prompted
the writing of this book. Thank you!
May our friendship last forever!

INSPIRED BY

"Every good and perfect gift is from above, coming
down from the Father of the heavenly lights, who does
not change like shifting shadows."
James 1:17
(NIV)

CHAPTER ONE

There was no way anyone could have predicted just how much Adam's life would change, neither could they have prepared him for it. It was to be the day that set the course of his life as God had ordained before he was even born.

With his eyes fixed on the slow-rising sun beyond the ocean's edge, he cupped his hands and dragged the crisp water back toward his waist, gliding the board beneath his body with ease to where he stopped just behind the last of the small breakers. He sat up, his feet dangling on either side of his surfboard and stared out toward the horizon. It was a beautiful early summer's day on the island, and as far as Adam was concerned, the best way to spend it. Soon his favorite surfing spot would be crowded by city dwellers who'd be arriving from all over the country. The island had always been a popular vacation spot, but he didn't mind it at all. Turtle Cove needed the business and The Lighthouse would have ample opportunity to carry out and continue its work. He loved seeing his church full. He smiled as he recalled how full the chapel had been during the previous year's summer. They were forced to pack more chairs out onto the grass and add extra speakers so everyone could hear his sermon. City folk from as far north as Massachusetts and Pennsylvania to Ohio and Tennessee had flocked to the island for the summer. He had much to be grateful for.

With his eyes closed and his hands stretched out toward the cloudless sky, he pushed his chin out and allowed for the day's first rays to flood his face. This had been his daily ritual for most of the twenty years he'd been living there. It was the time and place he had carved out to meet with God each morning while he watched the sunrise from behind the calm ocean waters. Alone in the water, he prayed out loud, praising, thanking God for his everlasting grace. His life on the island had been nothing short of incredible—more than he could have ever asked for. He had only been twelve when he came to live there. Why God had purposed it in that way, he still didn't quite know, but he had learned not to ask anymore. It's not for you to question God's motives, he reminded himself. The sudden tragic thought that forced its way into his prayers as it so often did broke his focus. His words trailed off as he allowed

2

his mind to enter the silent space where he waited for God to speak instead, something he urged his parishioners to do each time he took his place behind the pulpit. "In order to hear God speak you ought to be still in his presence," he'd say while quoting the psalmist. But today Adam's spirit was restless. Why he didn't know. He just couldn't connect the way he normally did. He dropped his hands and rested them on his thighs while he stared out across the ocean. The waves had died down and all was calm and quiet around him. Deciding to head back, he turned his board around and pointed its nose toward the beach. As he patiently waited for a wave to carry him in to shore, he glanced out toward the sand dunes in the distance. In the early dawn light, he spotted faint white smoke that trailed like a ribbon into the sky. He squinted his eyes to bring it into vision. A frown formed across his brows as he sat back up on his board. *It's coming from the mission. Could it be? What else? The Lighthouse was the only cluster of buildings out there. Ruth… Abigail… my girls!* Something clutched at his heart. His torso slammed flat onto the board. His arms and feet worked at three times the normal speed to push his surfboard through the quiet water toward the beach. He briefly turned to find a wave to help him. There weren't any. *Please, God, send me a wave. Just one big one, please, Father!* He kept pushing across the water as he kept his eyes fixed on the smoke that grew thicker with each passing moment. The smallest of waves lifted his board just enough to propel him into the surf. He kicked harder. As the ocean spat him out onto the shoreline he ripped the Velcro strap to release the leg cord from his ankle and left the board to be swept back into the sea. He couldn't be bothered with it right now. All he could think about was whether his wife and daughter were safe.

His feet sank into the soft white sand while he bolted across the beach to where the narrow path snaked between the grassy sand dunes. From behind the mounds, the white smoke that had turned dark gray towered into the sky. As he gained perspective over its location he had the sudden urge to hurl into the nearby bushes. He kept running and instead spat a ball of salt-water that had settled in the back of his tight throat into the sand in front of him. Some of it caught on his cheek but he didn't care. All he cared about now was Ruth and Abigail. The reminder of what was at stake injected a flood of adrenalin into his legs. It was enough to propel him over the last sand mound before he entered the grounds of the mission. But the surge of strength in his body was soon replaced with a sudden heavy feeling that had left his feet strained and weighted to the ground. What he had feared most suddenly punched him in the gut and left him breathless.

Oblivious to the plan that was about to unfold and alter his life in ways he never saw coming, Adam Cross charged toward his home. Smothered in a blanket of dark clouds of smoke that now oozed from between the logs of the cabin's walls, he fixed his gaze on the blazing fire. The sweet scent from the large magnolia shrub that normally permeated the air in front of their cabin was gone. His bare feet hit the small deck, which instantly melted the soft flesh beneath his toes. Cassie barked somewhere behind him. He darted back onto the grass in search of the old trainers she had claimed soon after they had brought her home from the shelter last Christmas. He scrambled to gather them up. They were in her favorite spot under the oak tree, next to Abby's swing. Barely conscious of the concerned cries that were now coming from the few community members who had since woken up, he slipped the shoes on, ignoring the gaping hole that left one big toe exposed. Back on the deck, the fire had engulfed the entire front portion of the house. His heart pounded hard against his chest and it didn't take long for his lungs to react and fight against the smoke that stung in the back of his throat. His eyes and nostrils burned under the relentless fumes that grew stronger with each passing second. Instinctively he buried his face inside the crook of his elbow. As his lips tasted the salty-foamed sleeve of his wetsuit he thanked God that he was at least insulated from the fire. The front door easily gave away under the thrust of his peep-toe trainer. Instantly the sudden additional supply of oxygen fueled the inferno and caused Adam to recoil onto the porch, shielding his face behind his neoprene arms.

"Ruth! Abby!" he yelled into the flames.

They must still be in their beds! He turned to head to Abigail's room first, coughing and choking in the smoke.

Once again a surge of adrenaline jolted his muscles into action, pushing through his veins like an electrical current. His pulse quickened to an unsteady pace he could no longer control.

He called out to his wife, barely recognizing the hoarse sound of his voice.

"Ruth! I'm here! Ruth!"

No one answered. All he heard was the loud crackling sounds as the fire ripped through his home. Behind him, a rafter crashed to the floor and narrowly missed his shoulder. Again he called out in the hopes of getting a response. First his wife's name, then his daughter's, but still there was no sound from either of them. As his mind raced and his body propelled forward toward their bedrooms, he silently cried out to God. *Make a way through the flames, Lord! Clear my path!* The thought of losing his wife and child was unbearable. As quickly as the thought entered his mind he pushed it aside. There was no time to give in to fear. God was helping him. As he entered the first of the two bedrooms his eyes searched through the smoke. It was Abby's room. The smoke was thick and he could barely see the bed. It took two seconds to leap across the floor to where Abby's pink bed covers had already caught fire. He reached out and yanked it off to expose an empty space where he had expected his daughter to be.

"Abby! Where are you, sweetheart? Daddy's here!"

When he couldn't find her, he turned and set off toward the master bedroom. *Maybe she crept into bed with Ruth.* It was something she liked doing lately. Sweat blurred his vision and he wiped his eyes with the back of his trembling fingers. Another four strides to their room.

"Ruth! Are you in here?"

Through the thick smoke, his eyes searched their bed. His wife's dainty feet poked out from beneath the sunshine yellow comforter.

"Ruth! Wake up! We've got to get out of here. Ruth!"

She didn't answer, nor did she move. Now at her side, he pulled the covers off and patted the space next to her in search of Abby. She wasn't there. Fear tore through his body. While his eyes continued to scan the room for his daughter, his hand gently slapped Ruth's hot face. He couldn't tell if she was breathing. From somewhere behind him he heard the roof shift just before a couple of rafters crashed onto the floor. There was no time. He had to get her out of there. He'd come back for Abby. He scooped Ruth's unconscious body off the bed and threw her over his shoulder. Bolting toward the exit, his eyes searched unceasingly for his daughter. Large orange flames had ripped into the dining room drapes and burned a massive hole in the roof above the kitchen.

"Adam! Over here!" a male voice called out to him.

Through the thick smoke, he glimpsed the caretaker's welcoming brown eyes and eagerly followed Jim's voice to where he stood in the doorway between clouds of brown smoke that all but completely obscured his vision.

"Take Ruth! I've got to find Abby!" he yelled as he dumped his wife into Jim's arms.

"No, Adam! It's not safe! The roof is about to come down any minute! The fire department is on its way!"

"Go, Jim! Get Ruth out of here! I have to find Abigail!"

Adam swung around and charged toward the kitchen but instantly regretted his spontaneous decision when the unstable floor beneath his body collapsed and one leg disappeared below the burning floorboards. Around him, the flames danced across the floor as it torched its way through the rest of the house. From his sunken position, he spotted Abby's lifeless body next to her doll's house in the far corner of the sitting room. In a reflex action, he pushed his hands down onto the floor to lift himself from the hole, which instantly sent a burst of pain through his palms. He screamed in response as he freed his leg and leapt across the room to Abby's side.

"I got you, baby girl! Daddy's here!"

Above them, the roof crackled under the inferno as it made its imminent collapse known. He scooped his daughter's motionless body into his arms, cradling her against his chest. Forced to pause as he searched for a way to escape across the collapsing floor, Adam pleaded with God to keep it intact and come to his aid. His eyes stung and he could no longer see clearly. There were flames everywhere he looked. Behind him a sudden loud bang came from the kitchen, warning him to get out before the gas cooker exploded. Out of options, he pinned his eyes on the exit. As if the world around him briefly paused a crisscross exit path unfolded between the falling rafters and the collapsing floorboards. Adam bolted across the fragile floor, following the pathway toward the front door that had all but completely been destroyed. He cradled Abby's tiny body and tucked her in between his arms moments before the thrust of the explosion deposited them on the other side of the flaming porch.

CHAPTER TWO

He didn't quite know how long he'd been unconscious, or where he had been when he counted the trees in his sleep, but when Adam slowly drifted back into the present, it all came flooding back. His mind recalled the fire and the explosion, and how it blasted him and Abigail from the inferno. He tried to speak but his vocal cords ached when he did. His eyes locked onto a single gray cloud directly ahead of him. It told him that he was lying on his back. Above his head, someone suddenly hovered over him. Something tight was around his neck and his hands felt as if they were gripping hot coals.

"He's back! Adam, can you hear me?" the voice came from the sudden shadow over his face.

He did and tried to answer, but still he wasn't able to speak.

"It's okay, don't try to talk. Just try to take deep breaths."

Abby! Ruth! He cried out in his mind.

He moved his right hand in search of his daughter's tiny fingers. When the search turned up empty and he discovered he couldn't turn or lift his head either, his eyes turned to find her.

"Your wife and daughter have been taken to Lady Grace hospital. Let's give you the care you need first, okay? You inhaled a lot of smoke. That's why you're having trouble breathing and speaking. Your hands have third-degree burns but apart from that, you appear to be fine. You're a very lucky man to have survived the fire and the explosion."

Luck had nothing to do with it.

Adam closed his eyes and started praying for Ruth and Abigail. He thanked God that he'd got them out in time, before the house exploded. He wanted to be there, with them, not here flat on his back next to the magnolia bush. He took a few deep breaths through the mask that covered his mouth. He had to speed up his recovery so he could get to the hospital quicker.

To his right, he heard the murmured prayers of his small leadership team. Daniel, whose prayers were always steeped in adoration, Stephen who somehow found gratitude in every situation, and Andrew who'd been the church intercessor for years. As a pastor, he couldn't have asked for a better team. As he listened to their prayers, he silently joined in. From a distance, he heard someone crying. Who? Why? He strained his ears that still rang from the explosion. It was Elsbeth. Why was she crying? She never cried. She was a rock, a stalwart whose faith could never be shaken. He turned his head to find her.

"No, no, just lie still. We put a brace on your neck, just to be sure there's no damage. We'll need to run a few X-rays at the hospital to fully clear you."

Adam squeezed his eyes shut. Partly to confirm the instruction, but mostly out of frustration because he was stuck there on the ground. He'd never felt more helpless.

Hurry. Get me to the hospital so I can see them.

As if they heard him, two medics crossed his arms on top of his chest before they flipped him onto one side then rolled him back over onto a stretcher. Moments later they carried him down the path, passing his praying elders and—*more crying women.*

"We're praying for you, Pastor. God be with you." Their emotionally-charged voices swept past him.

In the ambulance, he felt the needle in his arm. Then everything around him slowly faded away.

"HEY, THERE'S MY FAVORITE NEPHEW," THE FAMILIAR sound of his uncle's voice sounded gently in his ears as Adam came to.

"Hey, Uncle Ben. I'm your only nephew by the way," he said with a smile. His voice sounded croaky but at least he could speak. The neck brace was gone and so was the pain in his hands. He raised his hands to inspect them.

"Now, now, don't move too much or you'll have that shoulder pop out of place again in no time. It looks like you should be able to go home later today. By the Lord's grace, your arm isn't broken. In fact, apart from popping your arm from its socket, and the burns on your hands, you don't have a single broken bone or injury in your entire body. A miracle if you ask me. You should be back on that surfboard of yours in no time."

Adam smiled. The surfboard was probably halfway to the Atlantic by now. He turned to take in the empty space on the other side of his bed before his eyes searched the rest of the hospital room hoping to find his wife and daughter.

"Where are Ruth and Abigail?"

"The nurse said they are being taken care of and that the doctor would speak to us as soon as you woke up. They've been in and out of the room all day so I reckon they'll be here to check up on you again any minute."

Adam stared at the sling that supported his left arm.

"Are they okay?"

"I have no idea, Adam. They were taken into surgery as soon as they arrived at the hospital yesterday."

"Yesterday?"

"Yes, apparently you've been lights out since they drove you off. I took the first flight out of Tampa the moment I heard the news last night. Danny and the rest of the team have been taking care of things at The Lighthouse so don't you worry about a thing. We're all here for you."

His attention wasn't on the mission. Truth be told, it was the furthest from his mind. Of course his work was important to him, but right now, all Adam could think about and longed for was to see his beautiful wife's and daughter's smiles.

As if silently summoned, a nurse entered the room. Two steps behind her, a man wearing blue scrubs followed her in and stopped to read the clipboard at the foot of the bed, his stethoscope draped around his neck. Realizing it was the doctor, Ben jumped to his feet and started to nervously thread the brim of his yellowed Panama hat between his fat forefingers and thumbs. Sensing the pensive looks, the surgeon placed the chart back in its place, locked his fingers together in front of his abdomen, and stared down into Adam's searching eyes.

"Hello, I'm Dr. Bowden." He paused and then swallowed. "I'm sorry, Adam. We did everything we could for them. It was too late. There was nothing we could do. I'm very sorry for your loss."

No! This isn't happening! It can't be!

The doctor added something about smoke inhalation and the impact from the blast. His voice trailed off before his eyes met Ben's and then he quietly turned and left the room, the nurse behind him.

It's not real. This is a dream, a nightmare. Tell me this isn't real!

While the doctor's doom-filled words still echoed in his ears, Adam could barely breathe. From beneath the invisible elephant that seemed to push down on his chest, a similarly unseen fist had thrust itself between his ribs and ripped his heart out without permission.

Give it back! It's not yours to take!

Every emotion possessed by man flooded through his numb body all at once. Disbelief, anger, pain, nothing made sense. He wanted to cry, but he had no tears. Just an empty void where his heart had been.

"I'm so deeply sorry, Adam." His uncle's saddened voice cut through the silent room as he slumped into the chair beside the bed. "I'll stay for as long as you need me."

Adam ignored his uncle's empty words. He flung the sheet back and swung his legs over the side of the bed while simultaneously ripping the oxygen mask from his mouth.

"Where are you going?" Ben was on his feet again.

"I don't believe him. I want to see them. He's making a mistake. Ruth and Abby are not dead. He's got the wrong family."

Adam was halfway to the door already, clasping the open hospital gown on his rear with his bandaged hand.

"Adam, calm down. I don't think you should be out of bed just yet."

Ben trailed after him, the ball of his hat now gripped underneath an outstretched hand next to his side, his walking stick, meant to aid his bad knee, dragging behind him on the floor.

"Adam! Wait. Let me call the doctor." Ben struggled to keep up the pace.

But Adam ignored his uncle's plea as he hastily made his way toward the nurses' station at the far end of the hallway.

"Sir, you should be back in bed. You haven't been—"

"Where is he? The doctor that was just here. Where did he go?"

"Sir, you need to calm down, please."

Adam didn't wait and continued past the nurses' station to the big double doors marked 'Theater.'

"Dr. Bowden, this is an urgent call. Please come to Ward three. Dr. Bowden, please come to Ward three. " The intercom sounded overhead.

Adam's fingers closed around the door handle. It was locked. He yanked it back and forth before turning to look for a release button on the wall next to it.

"Adam, stop! Please. They've called the doctor. You need to stay calm." Ben was out of breath. In his seventies already and walking with a limp in his left leg he couldn't keep up with his thirty-two-year-old nephew's urgent pace.

Adam stopped. *The morgue.* He turned and headed for the elevator, pushing past his uncle.

"Now where are you going?"

"They're not dead, Uncle Ben. I'm telling you."

He jabbed his index finger on the down arrow several times before he stepped back and glanced at the illuminated floor numbers overhead.

"He's got the wrong family and I'll prove it. If they're dead they'll be in the morgue. I carried both of them out of that fire. They're alive." Adam slammed at the button with the flat part of his hand when the doors took too long to open.

"Mr. Cross, Adam," the doctor suddenly spoke behind him.

"Where are my wife and daughter? I want to see them. They're not dead. Do you hear me? You have the wrong family. My wife, her name is Ruth. Ruth Cross. And my little girl, she's seven. Her name is Abigail. She has long, curly blonde hair, like my wife's. They were taken to Lady Grace hospital." Adam's eyes searched for any name signs to confirm his bizarre theory that he had to have been brought to a different hospital.

"Adam, this *is* Lady Grace. Please, let's calm down first. I'll take you to see them," the doctor said calmly.

His words were exactly what Adam wanted to hear.

"So they are alive. I knew it. You made a mistake. That's fine, Doctor. We all make mistakes. Just take me to see them, please. I'm calm, I promise. I just want to talk to my wife and my little girl."

Adam caught the silent exchange between the doctor and his uncle just before Ben started rolling his hat's brim between his fingers again.

Lord, please let them be wrong. They don't believe me. They think I'm crazy. Let it be a mistake.

A nurse behind him held out an open robe and signaled for Adam to slip it on over his exposed derriere. He nodded, conveying his gratitude. He'd forgotten all about the gaping hole exposing his tan line.

"Please, follow me."

The doctor led them back down the hallway, past the nurses' station before he turned left down another corridor.

Adam followed with his uncle huffing and puffing close behind. The doctor paused at an elevator and scanned his ID card that he had pulled out from somewhere underneath his blue theater shirt. The door instantly opened. Adam's bare feet stepped onto the textured, steel floor with its multitude rhombus patterns that had him look down, skimming over his bandaged big toe. Amongst the hundreds of small patterns that stretched out beneath his feet, his eyes instantly picked out one of the patterns that was missing one of its sides. *A manufacturing flaw.*

"Adam, you're going to need to brace yourself. As a pastor, I'm sure you've seen many that have passed, but it's different when they're your own."

They're not dead.

The ping sound above his head signaled the door was about to open. In the back of his mind, a gentle voice whispered. *My grace is sufficient for thee: for my strength is made perfect in weakness.* He knew the voice. It was God's. And he knew the scripture too. It was the very one he had used at Natalie Johnson's vigil before she lost her long battle with breast cancer and had left a grieving husband and three young children behind. But this wasn't a vigil or a funeral. It wasn't the same. *Was it?*

He followed the doctor into a big open area and was told to wait in a small, narrow room with two chairs that stood along one wall. Moments later the doctor returned and ushered them into an adjoining room that, much to his surprise, didn't smell anything like a place where they opened up dead bodies. It didn't smell of death. Just strong cleaning liquids. He had never been inside a mortuary before.

A man wearing a green hospital mask and matching

gown that was tied at the back walked toward them. Carrying a large clipboard he beckoned for them to join him next to a wall of tightly packed silver doors. Adam had seen these on television. They looked exactly like the ones on *CSI*. His throat suddenly felt dry at the thought that Ruth and Abby might be in there. *No, they weren't. They're not dead.*

The coroner paused, casting a cautious eye at the doctor before he opened first one drawer, then a second next to it. Suddenly Adam's heart was back, thudding like a *Nutcracker* soldier's drum against his chest. Again he heard the same voice. *My grace is sufficient for thee...* At that moment, before the sheets were even pulled away, he knew what was to come. He knew he was about to see the lifeless faces of his beautiful wife and daughter. If this was God's grace he didn't want it. He could take it back.

And as Pastor Adam Cross wrestled with God and his unsolicited free gift of grace, he stared down at the pale, lifeless faces of his loving wife and sweet baby girl.

CHAPTER THREE

The mood at The Lighthouse was somber, as was to be expected. Most of the dozen missionaries had either been frequent visitors over the years or had remained there indefinitely and so Adam, Ruth and Abigail were like family to them. They had formed an emergency team to gather some supplies and clothing almost as soon as they were rushed off to hospital since everything Adam possessed had been lost in the fire. A few community members had offered their time and services to fix up and paint a derelict chalet that had been vacant and out of use for some time—as a temporary measure for the three of them to come back to.

There had been no news from the hospital yet and so they faithfully set about preparing for their return. But Elsbeth's episodes of crying didn't help any of them.

"Adam doesn't need this right now, Elsbeth. Pull

yourself together. We need to be strong for them. I'm certain they'll be back soon and this chalet is nowhere near ready." Daniel's tone was stern.

It wasn't his usual character but as the mission's elder, the moment had called for it. In all his time serving together, he'd never seen Elsbeth quite like this. She'd always been the mission's rock, the unshaken faith warrior who kept everyone rooted in their faith. Yet today, Elsbeth Porter was a ball of tightly woven yarn that had just come undone and lay frayed and scattered all over the floor.

He had always suspected that she had run from something or someone way back when she first arrived at The Lighthouse and then never left. But she'd never spoken about it, even though the two of them shared a closer than normal relationship. The kind of closeness usual between siblings or bosom friends, not couples.

Daniel paused over the mint-green comforter he had just spread out over the double bed when a message on his phone bleeped. It was from Ben. As his eyes skimmed over the short sentence that delivered the tragic news, he instantly fell to his knees next to the bed and stared into a dead space between the pillows.

"Danny?" Elsbeth nudged.

"Ruthie and Abby didn't make it. Adam's fine."

The words instantly sent Elsbeth into hysteric crying where it soon left her hyperventilating and unable to breathe.

Daniel rushed to where she had fallen back against the empty wardrobe where she'd been filling it with donated clothing. She buried her face behind her bony hands, looking tired and much more fragile than usual. Of average height, she'd always been thin, even though she could pack away food like there was no tomorrow. Even her ordinarily perfect bun in the nape of her neck suddenly looked disheveled. Daniel pulled her head against his shoulder. At about five foot six, it lined up perfectly with his five-eleven athletic frame.

"It's okay, Beth. It'll be okay." Daniel struggled to believe his own words. But they stood there for a while, consoling each other until it was time to let the others know.

"Take a deep breath, Elsbeth. You're going to have to calm down now before we tell the others."

"I'm sorry, Danny, I'm trying. Really I am. It's just, well, Adam's been like a son to us, you know? I feel like this is a twisted game of déjà vu. As if the clock has turned back and we're all right there again after that horrible incident twenty years ago. It's all just too much."

Daniel knew what she meant. He had thought it too.

"I know, Beth. None of us needs to be reminded of what happened. But just as we got him and all of us through that terrible time, we'll do it again. With God as our center. We're going to fully rely on God to help us, and especially Adam, through this horrific tragedy."

He peeled a still sobbing Elsbeth from his shoulder and held her at arm's-length, bending down until his hazel eyes made contact with hers.

"Take heart, my dear Beth. Just like Jesus tells us to do in John 16:33. He has overcome the world, and while we don't quite understand why he allows the suffering of this world, we know he uses it to build and strengthen our faith in him. One day we will look back and see God's hand in all of this. Let's praise his name and thank him instead. Adam was spared and, as certain as I am standing here, I know it will all work itself out."

And just like that, Daniel Reed did what he had always managed to do with anyone he came in contact with; he brought Elsbeth Porter to a place of peace.

***

IT SEEMED LIFE HAD BROUGHT ADAM CROSS FULL circle. There he was, broken, without purpose and alone, in the very place it had all begun. Sitting there alone in the dark chapel, staring at the image of Christ's tortured body pinned to a cross behind the very pulpit he'd been standing on every day for the past ten years, he had never felt more lost or alone. Empty words of jumbled prayers swirled in his head, none of which made any sense, not that it came as any surprise. He hadn't prayed since the day of the fire. Not once. Not even a quick conversation with God. He couldn't. Or maybe he didn't want to. He wasn't sure. All he knew was that he felt empty. And lost. He hadn't cried either. Not even when they pulled the sheets back and he saw them lying there, drenched in a cloud of chemicals instead of their sweet, feminine scent.

He glanced across the medium-sized chapel with its modest chairs and empty flower vases. In less than five hours the chapel's seats would be taken up by the towns-people mourning and paying their respects to—he couldn't even say their names. Not even in his head. Anger bubbled up and made him clench his jaw. It wasn't fair. None of this was fair. *Was God playing a cruel joke on him?* He stared at the anguished face of Christ reminding him of his own suffering on the cross. There was a time he felt Christ's pain, his suffering. But right now, he felt nothing. He was numb inside. His soul was dead. It had died in that fire along with them.

"I COULDN'T SLEEP EITHER." ELSBETH'S GENTLE VOICE surprised him when she took a seat in the row of chairs behind him.

"Sorry, I didn't mean to startle you. I wasn't going to come in, but... how are you doing?" Elsbeth clicked her tongue and shook her head. "I'm sorry. I don't know why I said that. It's a silly question. Don't mind me. I'll go sit over there."

She got up and started winding her way through the rows of chairs across to the opposite side of the chapel.

"I don't know if I can get through this," Adam whispered with no emotion in his voice.

His near-silent words stopped her dead in her tracks between two rows of chairs. Frozen on the spot she drew a deep breath before she turned to take a seat next to him. She didn't say a word. She had none. Instead, she drew him in a motherly embrace just like she had done since the day he came to live on the island. A role she happily stepped into and had never once regretted. She loved Adam with all her heart as if he were her own son.

"I know. It's okay. We'll find a way to get through this together."

Adam pulled back from her and stared into his lap. He didn't want to be consoled. He didn't want to feel anything.

"What if I don't want to?"

His words hit a familiar place that had been buried deep inside Elsbeth Porter's soul. She'd been in that place before, a very, very long time ago.

"You might not want to now, but you will again. You just need time."

They didn't speak after that. The two of them just sat there side by side in the quiet, dark chapel until the sun's first rays burst through the tiny row of windows that ran along the top of the east-facing wall and illuminated the sad eyes on Jesus' face—as if to once again draw their attention to the one who took upon himself the worst suffering of all so they could be set free. Except, he wasn't free. And neither was Elsbeth.

THE FUNERAL WAS SMALL AND INTIMATE WITH JUST their Lighthouse 'family' and a dozen of the town's locals who they'd come to know over the years. As with all the other small towns that were sprawled out along the US East Coast, the residents of Turtle Cove had all known each other.

The Lighthouse Church Mission had been an integral part of the community since the mid-1900s and as far as Adam was aware, it was also where his parents had met and fallen in love.

"My heart has just about fallen to pieces for you, Pastor Adam." The shrill voice and strong southern accent of the mayor's wife cut through the small gathering as she fought her way to the front of the short line to pay her respects.

"Ruthie's fine peach cobbler will leave a huge gap at next month's town fair. And your dear little Abigail. Oh, bless her precious heart. My Maribelle will sorely miss her company. It's all just too devastating," she continued, flapping her white-gloved hand in front of her false eyelashes, heavily powdered face and thin red lips.

"Thank you, Miss Carrie," was all Adam managed

to say before she stepped away to bury her nose in a white lace handkerchief.

The rest of the service was a blur. Daniel did as fine a job of delivering a decent eulogy as could be expected, but his words left little to no impact on Adam who stared blankly throughout the entire service. He didn't quite know how he got to the small graveyard that sat tucked between the edge of town and the National forest, but when they lowered the two ivory coffins side by side into the fertile ground, he caught himself staring up into the tall trees that seemed to pierce holes in the overcast sky. He had looked away intentionally. He couldn't watch them sink beneath the earth.

My grace is sufficient for thee: for my strength is made perfect in weakness. The words rang in his head. Over and over. He closed his eyes, squeezing his lids together as if trying to force it from his mind. It didn't work.

And when he finally opened his eyes again, sudden movement behind a nearby tree caught his attention. Probably a deer, he told himself when he looked and found nothing. Pleased by the welcome distraction, away from Miss Carrie's overbearing sobs behind him and the incessant scripture in his head, he focused his attention on the tree in the distance. There it was again. Ever so slightly, moving in the dark shadows behind the large pine tree. He squinted his eyes, pinning them on the shadowy outlines that now didn't look anything like a deer. A slight frown pulled his eyebrows closer together.

There, lurking, watching from the safe shadows of the tall green trees, as they lay his darling wife and daughter to rest, his eyes determined the unmistakable figure of a stranger hiding in the woods.

CHAPTER FOUR

I t had been two weeks since his soul left his body and his life shattered into a million pieces. And upon each new day that Adam woke he felt worse than the day before. His life had become dreary and pointless. Empty.

Where he'd once looked forward to hitting the ocean at the crack of dawn to meet with the one who gave him purpose, he now spent his time beside their fresh graves at the edge of the forest; wishing he was buried there too. He'd sit there for hours on end, staring at their headstones.

Both were upright and made of white marble laced with matching pink trim along the upper edges. In the center, Ruth had an image of a rose—she loved them— and Abigail's stone had an angel. Miss Carrie insisted her and the mayor take care of it on Adam's behalf—to spare him the agony. It was a relief if he was honest. He just couldn't face flipping through the catalogues as if he were picking out a present for each of them. A present neither would ever see nor enjoy. Besides, he had to hand it to Miss Carrie. She had impeccable taste. The headstones were understated yet dignified. It was exactly as Ruth and Abby would have chosen for themselves.

Spending his days seated next to their graves staring aimlessly into space had become his new normal. He would get up before the sun rose and walk the two miles along the beach to the edge of the forest with Cassie by his side. Never once did he look at the ocean waves. Never once did he pray either. He wanted nothing to do with the God he once spoke to, the God he once thought he knew. *Jesus Christ is the same yesterday and today and forever.* No, he's not! The God I knew wouldn't take my wife and daughter!

Adam grieved the loss of his beautiful wife and daughter, but he also grieved the loss of his purpose. He had nothing… no one to live for anymore. He couldn't bring himself to attend their daily prayer meetings or help serve meals at the local shelter. It was where Ruth had served the homeless each day. Where he could still hear her encouraging chatter. Where Abigail would help hand out cutlery. Everything at the mission seemed pointless and unfulfilling. The charred remnants of what had once been their joy-filled home were still there, a black pile of burned rubble in the shadows of the oak and Abby's swing. An eyesore in the middle of The Lighthouse grounds. There was nothing left. As if none of it had ever existed.

All that got him out of bed each day was the stranger between the trees. He had asked Daniel and Elsbeth if they saw him too, lurking behind the trees at the funeral. But they hadn't. No one did. Perhaps the stranger was a figment of his imagination. His mind playing tricks on him in a moment of distress. But Adam knew it wasn't. Deep down he knew what he'd seen that day, lurking in the quiet shadows. Who was he? Why did he hide? Did Ruth know him? Maybe he had started the fire, killed his wife and little girl. The questions gnawed at him. He needed to know.

Adam stared at the space behind the tree. The light summer shower had already soaked his thin sweatshirt and left him shivering to the bone. Cassie had taken shelter at the foot of a large tree where she patiently waited with him. Beneath Adam's crossed legs a muddy pool had already taken shape. But he didn't care. He'd wait there every day to catch the stranger if that's what it took.

"Adam?" Jim's gentle voice spoke behind him. Jim had been The Lighthouse caretaker for almost four decades. "They told me to come find you. You're soaked to the bone. You'll catch one of 'em nasty colds if you stay out here."

His wife had died from pneumonia five winters ago so it was a sensitive topic for him.

"Hey, Jim. I'll be all right. God would do me a favor if he took me."

"Nah, you'll get through this. Your wounds are still raw, that's all."

Adam shrugged his shoulders. He wasn't so sure. Even though he knew Jim's heart was once broken too.

"I've been meaning to thank you for what you did the day of the fire," Adam said.

Jim, who had crouched down to share his umbrella, turned to face him, his bushy gray eyebrows raised with curiosity.

"I'm not sure I know what you mean, Adam."

"For taking Ruth so I could go back to fetch Abby."

Adam noticed the blank expression on Jim's face. As if Jim had no idea what he was talking about. Sudden doubts filled his mind.

"Adam, are you feeling okay?"

Adam didn't speak his mind. *Am I okay? You're the one who looks like you've just seen a ghost.*

"Perhaps we should get you both in from the rain and get you some of Elsbeth's hearty chicken soup. Your uncle Ben's also waiting to say his farewells."

He summoned the golden retriever with a whistle and extended his hand to Adam. Accepting it, Adam slowly rose to his feet and jammed his hands into the wet pockets of his jeans. Was he losing his mind? Was he seeing things?

As they turned to head up to the clearing where Jim's muted green 1969 Ford pickup was parked, Adam stopped and turned to face him.

"Wait. You don't remember helping me that day, taking Ruth from me?"

Mildly amused, Jim let out a short puff of air through his nose.

"It's not that I don't remember, Adam. I *know* it wasn't me. I haven't been home for over a month. Remember? My little Lacey gave birth to another grandchild... in Atlanta. I drove up to meet my new grandson. He's a strong little fellow, I'll tell ya that. I bet he'll make a great player for the Falcons one day. Ira would have been so proud, God bless her soul." Jim chuckled with pride as he remembered his grandson and late wife.

But Adam hadn't heard a single word he spoke. Jim had lost his attention the moment he declared he'd not been home during the fire. Adam's mind was a flurry of questions riddled with doubt that left him out of breath. With his hands now on his hips he turned and started pacing back and forth haphazardly.

"Adam? Are you sure you're all right? I really think you should let me take you back now."

"It's impossible!" Adam blurted out loud. "I saw you that day, in the fire, inside my house! You were right there, next to me. I had just found Ruth in the bedroom but I had to go back to find Abigail. And suddenly you were there, in the entranceway. You took Ruth from my shoulders. You told me to get out before the roof came down! Don't you remember that?"

Adam was close to hysterical as he paced and scratched his head trying to make sense of it all. He was certain Jim was there. How else would they have made it out before the explosion?

"I wish I had been home to help you, Adam. I wish with all my heart I could have saved them. And I would have. It's when I usually do my rounds after you leave for your morning surf. I could have—" He turned and looked away.

Adam's mind suddenly recalled he hadn't seen Jim for at least a month. Every morning Jim would be outside by the time he'd stepped out onto the porch to go meet with God between the waves. Like clockwork, Jim would be there to greet him and give Cassie a pat. He was right. He wasn't there. And as Adam felt the sinking feeling of disappointment in his gut, his flat palms wiped the rain from his face and he drew in a deep breath before he slowly let it out.

"It wasn't your fault, Jim. You deserved to be with your daughter. Miss Ira would have wanted it that way."

As they walked to the pickup truck in silence, Adam's mind was a mess. Suddenly he didn't know anything anymore. Perhaps all of it was just a horrible nightmare. Perhaps he needed to take Daniel's advice and talk to someone that could help him through this. Maybe Daniel was right. Maybe this trauma had stirred something in his subconscious. Brought what had happened to him when he was twelve back to the surface, since he couldn't remember much of it anymore.

CHAPTER FIVE

lsbeth's slender frame hurried along the bustling sidewalk between the quaint shops in Turtle Cove. The bulk of the summer holidaymakers had already arrived and the stores were bustling with happy shoppers taking in the small coastal town's charming atmosphere. But as pleasant as it was to see the town come to life, it was the one time of the year when she was most afraid of being out and about.

She glanced back over her shoulder, something she did often whenever she was in town picking up supplies. It had become a habit almost without her realizing it. For twenty years Turtle Cove had been her saving grace and there wasn't a day that went by that she didn't thank God for bringing her there. But even in the knowledge and safety of more than twenty years' evidence of God's hand over her, she had never quite been able to entirely let go of her fears.

"Well good morning, Beth dear," Miss Carrie's shrill voice suddenly sounded behind her. It made her jump and Elsbeth let out a tiny shriek.

"Oh now, what's the matter? You look as nervous as a long-tailed cat in a roomful of rocking chairs."

"You just startled me, that's all."

"Well, it's only me, you silly girl. I was hoping I'd bump into you today."

"Why is that?"

"It's about dear Ruth, bless her sweet heart."

Miss Carrie placed one of her signature gloved hands on her chest. Why she wore gloves all the time, even in the peak of summer, no one ever quite understood. But her white lace gloves, blood-red lips and false eyelashes were synonymous with who Carrie Claiborne was. As the mayor's wife, a role she took very seriously, she felt it essential to look the part.

"Go on," Elsbeth prompted with slight trepidation.

She had known Carrie for a very long time and by now she already suspected she was about to be asked a favor.

"Well, as you well know, Ruth presided over our baking stand and the baker of the year competition at the annual town fair and she did such a delightful job. It sure is an immense loss to the entire community. No one has ever been able to beat her prized peach cobbler."

She paused and slipped her laced hand into her red leather clip purse and moments later pulled a black and white polka dot hanky out. She dabbed at the wet patches beneath her eyes and as quickly as she had retrieved it, clipped the hanky back into her bag along with her somber mood and straight away continued, sounding as cheery as ever.

"Now, I understand you're probably busier than a moth in a mitten with it being The Lighthouse's busiest time of the year 'n' all, but you would do this town the greatest of favors if you would find it in your heart to take over the baking stand at the fair." She paused, clasping her hands together in front of her chest like she had just won a prize, her bright red lips pulled up at the corners into a wide, open smile to reveal her perfect white teeth.

Elsbeth took a step back and nervously bit at her top lip. A million thoughts flooded her mind all at once. Ruth was a very dear friend and while it would be an honor to take her place, she wasn't sure she could do it. And she much preferred remaining in the background at these large events. She stared back at Carrie who by now stood bouncing up and down with excitement.

"Oh, I don't know, Carrie. I'm not much of a baker."

"But of course you are! I can't think of anyone Ruth would have take her place more than you. You would do her so proud. Besides, I'll help out where my time allows and I've already asked Mrs. Haywood if she'd help you. She might be old but her mind is still as sharp as ever. Not to mention that most of her bridge girls will be just too eager to take their chances at the first place. You'd hardly have to do any promotion at all. You will have a table full of baked goods before y'all can say tuck in. Come on, Beth dear. Do it for Ruth."

Elsbeth's eyes just about said it all in response to Carrie's purposefully played ace. It was a cheap shot and she knew it. But she was right. Ruth's commitment to the bake stand was an inspiration, to say the least. Just one of many roles she had taken on with a joyful heart.

"Fine, I'll do it. But just this once."

"Well, that just dills my pickle, Beth! Turtle Cove is ever grateful to you. Now I had better be off before the day's gone. I'll let Mrs. Haywood know. You have yourself a great day."

And as if a tornado had just whisked through town, Carrie Claiborne's black patent leather heels spun round and Elsbeth watched as she dashed across the street.

BACK AT THE MISSION, PREPARATIONS FOR THE SEASON'S first Summer Sunday Service were in full swing. Cordoned off from the main grounds, the youth ministry team was welcoming the kids who were attending the annual Sonkids summer camp and Elsbeth was relieved to see Adam chatting to a few of them.

"He must miss little Abby so much right now," Elsbeth commented to Daniel when he took a few of the grocery bags from her hands while they made their way across the lawns to the main kitchen.

"I would imagine so, yes. This is the first time I've seen him interact with anyone since the fire. Jim says he spends most of his time up at their graves. It really is so sad. He still hasn't been to any of our prayer meetings either."

Elsbeth sighed deeply.

"That's going to take time, a lot of time. And not even that will heal him completely."

The tone of her voice hinted that she somehow related to Adam's current state and made Daniel turn to look at her with curiosity. Aware of his inquiring gaze, Elsbeth busied herself with the vegetables in the pantry.

"I know exactly what will cheer him up a bit," she quickly redirected the conversation.

"I'll make us a large pitcher of sweet tea to have out there under the oak while we crack some code puzzles. He's always loved those."

Daniel gave a throaty chuckle.

"Now that's the best idea I've heard in a long time. He's still our reigning code breaker champion. Tell you what. I'll round up a few of the others and get the grill going while we're at it. It's exactly what all of us need right now."

THOUGH ADAM WASN'T IN THE SLIGHTEST BIT enthusiastic about the idea of being festive, especially since it had only been a short while since the tragedy, he found himself somehow persuaded by Daniel and Elsbeth.

"You know, Adam, it's okay to laugh again. No one's going to judge you. This is your safe zone, remember? Daniel's voice was gentle and warm as he pulled Adam to one side.

"Yeah, I know you're right. It's just... well, I feel like I'm betraying them. It's all just too soon. They should have been here." Adam's voice broke as his sadness wedged in his throat. "I just miss them so much, Danny. It should have been me dying in that fire, not them."

"What you're feeling has merit, Adam, but God uses everything to his glory. You should let him."

Pfft, God! He let them die!"

As if Daniel had read his mind he added, "I know what you're thinking, my boy, and I promise you, God didn't let them die. Sometimes bad things happen, and we don't understand why. I know you're angry right now, and it's even okay to be angry with God, but try drawing close to him. Rely on his supernatural strength to bring you through this."

I don't want to get through this!

Adam didn't tell him that he'd been secretly entertaining the idea of going away. He wanted, no needed, to get away from there. Everywhere he looked he saw Ruth's beautiful smile and warm brown eyes, heard Abby's joyful giggles as she played with her toys. He was even certain he'd seen them both dancing near the magnolia bush.

"Tell you what, let's leave your battle with God alone for a bit, just for tonight. You have a title to defend." Daniel pointed to the few members that had gathered under the tree.

"Look at them. They think they're going to beat you tonight. You're our code breaker champion, son. Go out there and show them you still have it."

Adam was fully aware Daniel was using reverse psychology on him, and he conceded. Right now, he needed the distraction.

IT WAS A BEAUTIFUL SUMMER EVENING AS THEY ALL gathered under the large oak tree. A fair distance behind them, the lot where the cabin once stood, had been cleared away. Since the investigation had been completed and nothing was left of it, there seemed no reason for anyone to be reminded of the horrific event that had left its mark on all who lived there. All that remained was Abigail's swing that dangled from the tree.

"You know we can take it down if you want," Elsbeth commented when she saw Adam staring at it.

He shook his head in reply. "It's all I have to remember her by. She loved that swing."

"Jim left a couple of boxes with a few things he found among the remnants when he cleaned up. I had him put them in my cabin for when you're ready to go through them. And I thought you might like this." Elsbeth handed him a brown paper bag she retrieved from underneath her chair.

"What is it?"

"Just something I thought you might need. To help you through."

Adam slipped one hand into the bag. He recognized it instantly as he pulled it out.

"Where did you find this?" he gasped.

"Ruth must have forgotten it at my house the night before the fire when we had our women's prayer meeting."

Adam ran his fingers over the gold embossing. At that moment he felt his heart would break all over again. It wasn't like Ruth to leave anything behind, ever. Are you trying to tell me something, Lord? he whispered in the stillness of his heart as his eyes skimmed over the words.

It was the first time he had spoken with God since the fire. The first time he'd acknowledged that God might be talking to him. The first time he paused to let him answer.

"I was waiting for the right time to give it to you." Elsbeth knew the timing couldn't have been more perfect the instant she spotted Adam's face.

Overcome with emotion, a lonely tear escaped from his eyes and Adam allowed himself to cry for the very first time since the fire. Right there, beside Abigail's swing and the large black patch of burned grass on the far end, he sensed his Savior's presence. It was as if God had given him a nudge, the softest gentlest of pokes in his broken heart just to remind him that He was still there.

> In all things God works for the good of
>   those who love him,
> who have been called according to his
>   purpose.

And when later on that evening Adam was alone and lying in his bed, he pulled the gift to his chest and allowed the gold words on Ruth's Bible to penetrate his soul and start healing his broken heart.

CHAPTER SIX

The annual Turtle Cove Summer Fair was buzzing with visitors almost as soon as the day broke. For the most part of fifteen years, it had been one of the town's biggest seasonal events and a major draw for those holiday seekers who partook in the annual East Coast sailing competition. As the halfway checkpoint in the race, the island soon became the coast's hidden gem among the barrier islands, bringing in the town's biggest trade.

It was also the single most important event in Carrie Claiborne's calendar.

Dressed in her typical personal spin on fifties fashion flair, she was even more amped than usual as she ran between the stalls to add what she called, her 'Claiborne touch.' Clipboard in hand, her nervous energy was infectious but if there was anything the mayor's wife did well, then it was organizing a carnival. And as if she needed to channel her inner power just to make sure she got through her enormous checklist, her usual white lace gloves had made way for a blood-red pair that matched a bright red neckerchief. And when Carrie Claiborne wore red, everyone knew she was performing at her peak and that it was best to stay on her good side.

"That boy is as useful as a steering wheel on a mule," she commented to Lottie Montgomery, who owned the town's beauty salon as she passed the games table. "I don't know why we still put up with him. His father swears he's good for more than washing cars, but I'm not so sure. He keeps messing up with the raffle tickets."

Lottie flicked her coiffed bleach-blonde hair over her shoulder while she prepped her stand's nail bar and pamper parlor.

"Perhaps you should let someone else take over the tombola this year and have him sit on the dunking chair instead," she laughed. "I know of quite a few people who'd like to toss that ball."

"You know what, Lottie, that's precisely what I'm going to do. You're a genius!"

"You're welcome," Lottie replied and popped a bubble of bright pink gum between her lips as she watched Carrie dash off.

She flew like a butterfly from table to table, flashing

her pearly whites as she greeted a few familiar holiday-makers along the way. There wasn't one Turtle Cove resident who wasn't indebted to her in one way or another. She'd single-handedly turned the town into a bustling coastal holiday hotspot and everyone who knew her well enough knew she was the proverbial successful woman behind her husband. With her exceptional ability to remember every name that crossed her path, clearly a heavenly gift that she did with the utmost of ease, she was well-loved and respected by all.

"Ah, Pastor Adam. Just the man I was looking for." She paused where Adam was dropping off a few more trays of baked goods at Elsbeth's baking stand. "I know you're running around like a chicken with its head cut off, but you'd do me the greatest of favors if you could find Doc Grady. There's already a line as long as the Mississippi at his kissing booth and the man's nowhere to be found."

Adam smiled.

"Our doctor *is* the most eligible bachelor south of the Mason-Dixon, Miss Carrie, so it's no wonder the people are lining up. Perhaps he saw the line and got cold feet," he laughed.

Carrie placed one hand on Adam's shoulder.

"It's so nice to see you smile again, Adam. No person should ever have to go through something so tragic, but I know our good Lord is watching over you, and if you ever need—"

She stopped mid-sentence as her eyes suddenly caught something over his shoulder. It was Doc Grady talking to one of the town's retired folk.

"There he is! Got to go grab him before he disappears again!"

And just like that Carrie whisked herself off to chase after the good doctor.

"This fair would be a complete flop without Carrie Claiborne," Elsbeth commented. "In fact, I'd venture to say Turtle Cove would be nothing without her. I don't know where she gets her energy from but our town couldn't have asked for a better wife for our mayor. To this day I still wonder where he found her."

"Yep, she's really been a strength. Now, speaking of strengths, you seem to be doing really well here too. I know Ruth is smiling down on you today. You've done her proud, Elsbeth. Thank you."

"You're being too kind, Adam. She's left behind a gaping hole that can never be filled. We all miss her, and little Abigail. I'm just glad to see you're doing better. You know we'll get through this again, just like we did all those years ago."

Adam tucked his hands into the pockets of his faded jeans and turned his gaze out toward the fairgoers.

"Yeah, I'll be honest though, Elsbeth. I don't recall much of what happened. I've been trying. Lord knows I've been trying to remember, but I just can't. It's like my memory has blocked it out or something." He popped one of Elsbeth's famous coconut ice squares in his mouth.

"Perhaps that's how God intends it to be, Adam. What's done is done. We can't change any of it so there's no point pondering on it. By the grace of God, your life was spared, twice now, and that's got to tell you something."

Daniel's jovial voice behind them interrupted their conversation.

"Here you are. Not that I'm at all surprised. I should've known I'd find you hanging around the baked goods. You've never been able to resist that sweet tooth of yours. Think you can tear yourself away?" he asked Adam with a slight mocking tone in his voice.

"I'm sure my waistline will thank you. What's up?"

Daniel draped his arm around Adam's shoulders as he ushered him to a more private spot away from the stall.

"We've been reflecting, and stop me if you think you're not ready, but we believe you've come a long way since the accident. So we thought you might appreciate a little fishing trip out at Cedar Creek. Just the guys. With the fair out of the way, we could all do with a little distraction away from everything. You've been through a lot and maybe it's time to watch the sunrise again. Two days, that's it. The women can hold the fort and we'll be back in time for Sunday's service." He paused, waiting for Adam to respond.

Adam chewed at the inside of his cheek. *Get away from it all. Who says I want to?* But he knew Daniel was right. There wasn't a day or a single second something or someone didn't remind him of what he'd lost. For as long as he could recall, he had watched the sunrise each morning, praising God for his goodness. But now, after the accident, it only reminded him of that morning. Getting away for a few days might be just what he needed. Not to forget his beautiful wife and daughter, but to forget that he wasn't there to save them.

"Okay, I'm in."

"Excellent. I'll let the guys know. And who knows, maybe you'll be lucky enough to be the one to catch our dinner." He let out a laugh.

ADAM SPENT THE REST OF THE DAY AVOIDING THE curious gazes from some of the regular holidaymakers who had since come to find out about the fire. Several had stopped him to share their condolences from whom he respectfully tried to escape as quickly as possible. He had expected to be stopped by a handful of Turtle Cove regulars who'd made the town their annual escape over the years, but he wasn't quite prepared for just how many of them eventually did. So when he saw an opportunity to escape the onslaught of questions, he didn't hesitate to take it. Seeking solitude in the furthermost corner of the large public parking area that led up to the nearby pier, he sat in the shade of a large pine tree, flicking a few loose white pebbles into a nearby open parking space. A fair distance away from the festival, it was quiet and peaceful, and the fresh ocean air that wafted between the sparse trees that separated the car park from the beach calmed his soul.

Somewhere behind him, a branch snapped and he turned toward where the sound had come from. There was nothing there. He ignored it, writing it off to likely be a scavenging seagull. He flicked another pebble against the nearby trashcan. It was already quite late in the day and the sun had started making its descent behind the calm ocean on the other side of the acreage behind him. Apart from a small crowd who had remained in the beer garden, the fair was slowly quieting down and for the most part drawing to a close, leaving the parking area nearly empty.

Deciding the coast would most likely be clear from sympathy bearers and that he should head back to help Elsbeth pack up her stand—and see if there were any of her delicious baked goods left—he jumped to his feet. Again a branch snapped behind him, this time it was closer. The noise sent an eerie feeling down his spine. Foxes didn't usually come this close to the pier so he ruled them out as well. On the other end of the sandy allotment that was roughly the size of a football field with a dozen sparsely placed pines scattered throughout, the beach lay deserted and quiet since it had been closed off due to the fair and the sailing competition. His eyes squinted against the bright pink and orange backdrop as the sun set over the ocean behind the trees. He stood firm, letting his eyes search the spaces between the trees in an attempt to see what had caused the noise. Overcome by a sinister feeling that he was being watched, he eventually called out.

"Who's there?"

No one answered. Again a branch snapped, this time it was over to his left. He thought of turning around to run, but something glued his feet to the spot.

"Is someone there?" he called out again, and this time he could just about make out the faint shadow of a tall figure between two trees. It was too far for him to see who it was, but there was no mistaking it. Standing there, in a small clearing with every intention of being seen, was a person. Behind him the ocean glistened in the last rays of the sun, fully exposing the clear outlines of a man wearing a long dark coat.

"Who are you? What do you want?" Adam yelled, the nervous tension evident in his voice.

The man didn't answer.

Could it be the stranger from the funeral? Suddenly convinced that it was he, Adam set off toward the stranger, keeping his eyes pinned on his slim shadowy figure.

"What do you want? Why were you at the funeral?" he shouted again.

But still the man didn't answer. He just stood there, facing him. Unmoving, rooted to the earth.

Adam increased his pace. His heart pounded hard against the inside of his chest. His throat dry, his hands trembling with fear, he never once let the stranger out of sight. Then suddenly the man turned and walked toward the beach. Again Adam increased his pace. Now in a slow jog, he followed the man between the trees, but the stranger walked faster too.

"Wait! Who are you? Tell me who you are? Why are you stalking me?"

But the man ignored him, and suddenly, like a mist before the sun, the stranger disappeared.

"No! Come back!" Adam yelled. In a frantic attempt to stay on his trail he spun around, searching through the trees in every direction. But the man was gone. Adam ran out onto the beach, as fast as his legs would let him. In the distance he spotted him, running along the beach.

Adam didn't hesitate and bolted after him, once again pinning his eyes on his stalker. *How is it he's gained so much distance?* As his body heaved forward, pushing through the thick, loose sand, straining to catch the stranger, Adam's feet failed him and he suddenly fell headlong, face first into the sand. Knocked dizzy and out of breath he lifted his head, not willing to give up just yet, but it was too late. He'd lost him.

CHAPTER SEVEN

E lsbeth tossed and turned. She had been restless for most of the night. Waking up on the hour wasn't anything out of the ordinary though. After all this time she had become used to not sleeping well, but tonight was somehow different. Her dreams were more intense, more vivid than ever before. Why, she wasn't sure, but it had been a slow buildup since the local paper printed the tragic news of the fire. It was as if fear crawled up on her, waiting to surprise her when she least expected it.

She had already woken up several times during the night, sweating and scared senseless, convinced she had heard footsteps on her porch. And since Cassie had gone with Adam on the fishing trip, the absence of the mission's communal canine alarm system that she had come to rely on over the years had robbed her of the security she so desperately craved.

A dull thud woke her up with a jolt and she sat up in her bed. Clutching her pillow, she nervously leaned back against the headboard, waiting, listening. She kept the lights off, relying only on the soft moonlight that pushed through her sheer curtains. Next to her, the bright blue digits on her alarm clock showed 4:00 a.m. She quickly turned to check if her window was still shut, relieved to find that it was. Through her lightweight cotton curtains, the light of the full moon nearly lit her entire room. It brought her some relief. Her eyes scanned the small room, stopping to focus on the shadow in the corner next to her dresser. It was just a shadow from the tree outside her window. Even with the window closed the sound of the ocean roared louder than usual; it was a spring tide. She wiped a bead of sweat from one eye using the inside of her nightshirt. Her cozy cabin's basic layout allowed for an almost full view of the front door from where she was in her bed, so she fixed her eyes on the windows on either side of it. She had shut all the windows earlier that night and it was hot and stuffy in her chalet. Her throat was dry so she reached for the glass of water on the pedestal and took a sip, never once breaking her gaze away from the door or the windows. As she placed the glass back on her nightstand she accidentally bumped her Bible to the floor. Biting her top lip she prayed the noise didn't draw attention to her. But to her relief, everything remained quiet, except for her heartbeat that thumped loudly in her ears. When, after several minutes, she still didn't hear anything out of the ordinary, she bent at the waist and leaned over the side of the bed to pick up her Bible. It had fallen open and lay face down on the floor, half-tucked under the night-stand. A bookmark had slipped out and her eyes glanced over the scripture that lit up in the moonlight.

When I am afraid, I put my trust in you.

She shut her eyes and repeated the words in her heart, clinging to every word as she slipped back down beneath the covers, clutching her Bible against her chest. As the enemy often did to pull the faithful back into a place of fear, her mind wandered to the previous day at the fair. There was a moment when she was certain she had spotted him among the crowds, looking for her, his blond hair curling out from beneath that red baseball cap he always wore. Fear gripped her heart. "No!" she shouted into the dark, "I will fear no evil, for you are with me; your rod and your staff, they comfort me. All the days of my life!"

And as Elsbeth lay there in the silence of the night, fighting against the fear that had haunted her every night since the day she'd left the city more than two decades ago, she eventually prayed herself back to sleep.

. . .

WITH THE MEN AWAY ON THEIR FISHING TRIP, APART from Jim who had already started his daily rounds securing the perimeter, The Lighthouse was quiet. The fair was over and out of the way and because it was also midweek and the young had left for their adventure camp, it meant they not only had an extra hour or two to sleep in, but they were now also relieved of their breakfast duties. The timing of the men's fishing trip could not have been more perfect since it freed the women up for some much needed personal time. So they had agreed to each go their own way that morning and meet up for an afternoon cup of coffee and a slice of lemon meringue pie at The Beans 'N' Cream Café in town. Elsbeth was relieved, deciding to use the time for gardening.

It was precisely the solitude she so desperately needed. She needed the time to pray. The time to figure out why she'd suddenly been so filled with fear. Was she sensing danger? Was God warning her? Or was it the devil sneaking in to deceive her. She couldn't let him... she wouldn't. Turtle Cove was the only place she felt safe and there was no way he'd ever find her there. She had made certain of it. While she kneeled next to the flowerbed to clear out some weeds her shoulders felt burdened as if they were weighted down by something. She was tired. Tired of hiding.

"You okay? You look like you haven't slept a wink."

Mary-Jo plopped herself down next to her and busied herself with a garden trowel.

"Yes, yes, I'm fine. Must be the heat," Elsbeth answered, which started a casual conversation about the unusually hot weather that had arrived early. Mary-Jo was in her mid-twenties and had been volunteering her summers at the mission since she left school. Her uninvited effervescent presence annoyed Elsbeth, but she held back from telling her and put up with her chatter. Elsbeth watched the girl's long, tanned arms move nimbly through the soil and couldn't help thinking how innocent life was at that age. She was reminded of her twenties and how naive she was. *Or just plain stupid!* If only she could go back and do it all over again. She'd have been married with at least three kids and half a dozen grandkids by now. It was a regret she still found hard to let go of. Elsbeth pushed the thoughts from her mind. She had much to be grateful for. She had Adam and even though he wasn't her own, she had loved him with all her heart from the first day he and his parents came to the island. What happened to him was awful but there wasn't a day she didn't selfishly thank God that he had given her a son to love as if he were her own. And the joy she felt the day Abigail was born was one she likely would never experience again. Her life was full of grace; yet, here she was, still living in fear, unable to get away from her past.

"Miss Elsbeth, you haven't heard a single word I said. Are you sure you're okay?"

Mary-Jo's voice cut through her thoughts.

"Oh, yes, dearie, I'm so sorry. How rude of me. Perhaps I should run up to the house and get something to drink. I think the heat is just getting to me today."

And before Mary-Jo could argue—or interrogate her as she so often did when her curiosity got the better of her—Elsbeth dashed across the lawns. When she got to her front porch she tossed her sunhat on the deckchair and reached to open her front door, catching her heart in her throat when she saw that the door stood ajar. Panic flooded her veins. She didn't move, didn't know what to do. She knew she had closed it behind her earlier. Her legs were paralyzed, stuck to one spot as she stared through the narrow opening into her chalet. She couldn't remember the scripture that had brought her solace the night before, sending another wave of fear up her spine. She squeezed her eyes shut. *Lord, help me!* She had no idea how long she stood there, frozen to one spot, but when courage finally came upon her and she managed to draw enough oxygen into her lungs to keep her from fainting, her hand slowly moved toward the door. The rustic wood stung her trembling fingers as if it had injected her with poison. The same poison that suddenly sat bitter on the back of her tongue. How did he find her? She'd been so careful. Why now, after all these years? Familiar feelings she had worked so hard to bury instantly flooded to the surface. She thought of running but she had already stepped over the threshold. Her eyes frantically searched through the cabin's interior. There was no one there. That left only two places he could be: the bathroom or her bedroom. The floorboards beneath her feet groaned under her fragile frame. She drew in a sharp breath and remained fixed to the spot. Listening. The sudden thought that he might be behind the door waiting for his chance to pounce on her had her heart skip three beats. Her hand went to the small gold cross around her neck, rubbing it between her trembling forefinger and thumb. An unexpected noise came from the bathroom and sent a fresh surge of fear through her legs. Every cell in her body was on high alert, tingling, burning, filling her with dread. She swallowed, annoyed at how loud it suddenly sounded. Whether it was curiosity or Mary-Jo's naivety that had rubbed off on her she didn't know, but she found herself moving toward the bathroom, unable to stop herself. *You stupid woman! What are you doing?* She knew she'd be exposed, vulnerable, powerless if she came face to face with him, just like all those years ago. But somehow, at that moment, with God's strength, she believed she'd be able to withstand him. She was older now, stronger. As she slowly walked toward the bathroom, her eyes caught sight of the kitchen knives on the countertop. She didn't hesitate and dashed to draw one from the block. Armed with earthly strength and superficial courage, she held the knife out in front of her. Her knuckles lay white against the black handle, her skin in a cold sweat. She was certain she smelled his cheap cologne. It was a stench she'd never forget. She felt sick to her stomach. Moving closer, one featherlike foot at a time, her heart raced against her chest. She tried to calm her nerves by praying but all her favorite scriptures had escaped from her mind. All she felt was terror. Another sound echoed from the bathroom, instantly jolting her to one side. He was waiting for her. Waiting until she was close enough. So he could hurt her again. *Not this time! Not today!*

She tightened her fingers around the carving knife, locked her elbow so her arm extended firmly out in front of her. When she was ready she leapt the last few feet and burst into the bathroom, waving the knife as if she was swatting a fly, screaming at the top of her lungs like the Romans did when they attacked their enemies. She heard his cries, crying for her to stop. Saw his tall body tower over her before his big hands grabbed the knife from her and threw it to the floor.

"No! You're not going to hurt me! Get away from me!" Her body had lost all fear. Today she would fight, with everything she had in her.

"I'm not going to hurt you! Elsbeth, calm down! What has gotten into you?"

In the distance, her mind recognized his voice, but she didn't stop. She slammed her fists into his chest, never once looking up into those eyes. The eyes that used to tell her how pathetic she was. The eyes that showed what a disappointment she was. The eyes that told her he was the one in charge.

She heard the voice again. The voice told her to open her eyes. She tried to resist the instruction but couldn't. She was too weak. He'd won... he'd won.

CHAPTER EIGHT

B ut the eyes she saw weren't the ones she'd expected to see. With her wrists gripped between his strong hands, she stared up into eyes filled with confusion and questions. She wasn't sure if she felt relieved or angry. Did she want it to be him? So she could kill him. So she could finally live out her days without fear. At that moment Elsbeth realized her heart was filled with hatred. She hadn't forgiven him. She hadn't forgiven herself. Defenseless against her raging emotions she allowed her body to relax and tears freely flowed down her flushed cheeks.

"There we go. You're okay. I've got you, Elsbeth. I'm not going to hurt you. No one is here to hurt you."

Jim let go of her hands and ushered her back into the kitchen where he set her down at the small four-chair dining table. When she had downed the glass of sugar water he had given her she spoke for the first time.

"What are you doing here, Jim? I thought you were… I thought you were an intruder."

Jim, who had sat in the chair opposite her, answered her in the gentlest of tones.

"I was fixing your tap in the shower, remember? You asked me to have a look at it, last night when we were having dinner." He paused then spoke again. "Is everything okay, Elsbeth? Who did you think I was?"

Elsbeth sat frozen in her chair, staring at Jim as he explained his presence. She couldn't remember asking him. Yet, there he was. And she did have a leaking tap in the shower. Was she losing her mind? She moved out from behind the table and briskly walked over to the kitchen sink. Her fingers were still trembling as she opened the tap and ran water into her cupped hands. It was cool and sobering when she splashed it over her face. Afterward, she stood there staring into the empty sink, her back turned to him, feeling like such a fool, before she finally spoke.

"I'm sorry, Jim. I don't know what came over me." *Fear came over you! You're a Peter. You sank between the waves!* She recalled the story of when Jesus called Peter to walk to him on the water. Had she lost her faith? Had she allowed the enemy to steal her faith?

"Why are you so afraid, Elsbeth? What's going on? Talk to me, I can help you."

Jim was a good man. He had been at The Lighthouse since before she even came there. They were the same age and they'd been friends ever since. She was there for him when his wife died. She knew she could trust him. Still something inside her fought against it. She couldn't trust anyone. Not with this.

"I'm fine. It's nothing. The heat just got to me, that's all."

"It's not the heat, Elsbeth, and you know it. You almost killed me back there."

Elsbeth buried her face in the tea towel she had fumbled between her thin fingers.

"I know, Jim, and I'm really sorry. It was nothing but a moment of temporary insanity. I'll be all right."

She hung the tea towel back on a tiny hook on the wall and straightened her hair, collecting herself.

"Did you manage then?" she asked as if nothing had happened.

Jim rose and placed his big, callused hands on his hips.

"What?"

"The tap. Did you manage to fix it?"

She busied herself with washing out the sugar water glass.

"If you think your life is in danger, Elsbeth, you ought to tell me. We don't need another incident on our hands."

Jim's words stung as she stood at the sink. The tone in his voice added suspicion to his words.

"What do you mean *another incident*? The fire was an accident. What does that have to do with what happened here today?"

She had turned to face him now.

"I'm just saying. Things happen, and if there is a way to prevent it, we should."

Elsbeth's questioning eyes held Jim's in a firm grip. He knew he had said too much. That she was smart enough to know he was hiding something.

"Spit it out, Jim. What do you know?"

Jim drew a deep breath through his nose and held it in his lungs for a brief moment before he let it go.

"They don't think it was an accident. They think it was started deliberately."

His words left her cold and she stared at him, now leaning her backside against the sink.

"What are you saying, Jim? Someone killed them?"

"We don't know. Not for certain. But it looks that way."

"Why would someone want to kill Ruth and Abigail? They've never said or done anything to anyone. She was a child for goodness' sake!"

Elsbeth caught her breath.

"Unless—" She didn't finish her sentence. She didn't need to. Jim had reached the same conclusion the moment they told him.

"Does Adam know?" She knew it was a silly question to ask since he was away on the fishing trip.

Jim shook his head. "Not yet. I don't know if I should even tell him. Chief Perry only let me know this morning. You're the only one I've told."

Elsbeth shook her head in disbelief.

"Who would want Adam dead? This doesn't make any sense."

Jim shrugged his shoulders.

"I don't know, but I'm not sure we should tell him, or anyone else for that matter. Not until the chief has conclusive evidence. I've tightened up on the security and I have guys installing a fence down by the beach later today."

He caught the look on Elsbeth's face. It was very evident she was relieved to hear about the additional security measures. But he decided not to query her on it for fear of sending her off on another tangent. Deciding to focus on his own secret, for now, he forced her eyes on his.

"You can't tell anyone yet, Elsbeth. Not until we know what we're dealing with. For Adam's sake."

Her gaze met his.

"I won't tell anyone if you don't tell anyone either."

Jim knew she wasn't referring to the fire. Her eyes had made that clear.

"Fine. I won't tell anyone how you almost killed me

today, but if you suspect something that could put the mission in danger, you tell me. Got it?"

"Got it."

ADAM LAY STARING AT THE NEAR FADING STARS through the netting of the tiny skylight in his tent. With his internal clock habitually wired, he had woken up just before sunrise. No matter how hard he fought it, he'd wake up like clockwork every morning as he had done for nearly a decade. It was as if God was nudging him to rise and go to the place he had always met with him each morning—between the crisp ocean waves where the sun's warm light brushed his face. He sat up, his shoulders slumped forward and his head in his hands. It had been nearly three months since the accident and he hadn't been able to face God yet. He couldn't. He had so many questions that remained unanswered. Why did God let it happen? Why did they have to die? What did he do to deserve this? The lyrics of one of his favorite songs suddenly ran in his head. It spoke of suffering and pain, and turning it into praise. Of gratefulness in times of trouble, and clinging to hope even when you're crushed beyond what you can bear.

The words played in a loop in his head. Just three months ago his world was all it should be, and he'd praised God for it every morning. For his grace and his mercy. For the blessings he poured out on him. For his heart that overflowed with joy. But now his road was marked with suffering. The Lord had given and he had taken away. He was a pastor of a great church, a mission ordained to teach others about God's mercy and love, yet he couldn't turn his own suffering into praise. He couldn't sing the words to the song he had belted out so often. His mind jumped to Job. How did he do it? How did he praise God in the midst of his suffering? *Job never lost faith. He kept his eyes on God. He put God first. He trusted him.*

Adam's heart was heavy. His spirit conflicted. The words echoed loudly in his mind. He knew what he had to do. There was no more running. No place he could hide.

As if driven by an unseen force, he unzipped his tent and stepped out into the crisp early morning light that peeked through the tall trees. The sun would be up very soon. Around him the other men were still asleep, their camping spot quiet. God had provided the perfect opportunity. Now, it was up to him. He didn't hesitate and set off toward the water. His bare feet hit the trail with urgency. He needed to get there before the sun came up. It didn't matter that it wasn't on his surfboard. It didn't matter that it wasn't out in the open ocean. All that mattered now was that he got to the inlet on time. He had an appointment, a spiritual meeting he couldn't miss.

He ran faster down the hill toward the water's edge, his body pushing forward. His torso leaning further than his legs allowed. The sharp edges of tree roots sliced into the soles of his feet. A branch smacked him across his cheek, leaving a burning sensation in its place. Still he didn't care.

Nearing the small clearing at the water's edge, he briefly looked up. The sun just about peeked out from behind the horizon and cast its early rays across the tranquil water. This was why he loved Cedar Creek so much. As far as he was concerned it was the golden pathway that led directly east before it opened up to receive the most glorious sunrise known to mankind. His heart leapt with joy. His heart thumped against his chest and he found himself properly smiling for the first time since the accident. He was almost there. He'd meet with his Savior again. He'd be able to ask for forgiveness, receive his mercy. Thank him for his grace. Surrender his heart, his suffering, his guilt.

Just about at the water's edge, he leapt over the final few yards ready to dive into the creek. In a brief moment, when the water just about touched his feet, his weight propelled his body off balance. His legs tried to catch up. His arms flailed like two flags in the wind. A jolt of adrenalin momentarily froze all his internal organs as his brain warned him of what was to come. As if he watched his body from somewhere high above his head, he saw how his right foot hit the edges of a large round rock that was covered in moss, moments before it slipped off and wedged sideways, slamming his body flush with the water's surface. The crisp water hit the back of his eyes and pushed into his nose and mouth, almost at the same time as he felt something hard slam against his head just above his right temple. In the short moments between consciousness and his subliminal mind, his body felt weightless as the water swept over it and slowly pulled him under. Then suddenly, everything around him went dark.

CHAPTER NINE

I n the distance, a bright light beckoned him to go toward it. He saw Ruth and Abigail, their arms stretched out to him, their hair glistening in a golden light. Abigail was calling his name, her big smile exposing her two missing front teeth. The light lured him to join them. Oh, how he wanted to hold his little girl again. See his wife. But something was holding him back. He couldn't go forward. He cried out to Ruth to take his hand, to help him. Somewhere to his right, he heard his mother's gentle voice. He turned to face her. Her eyes were as blue as the last time he stared into them before the car crashed in between the trees. He called out to her. Where was his father? He looked around for him but couldn't see him. Ruth and Abby were slowly fading, withdrawing into the bright light. No! No, come back, his mind cried out.

Then his mother's voice spoke again. "Adam, go back. It's not your time yet. Go back! You need to find it and set him free."

And as all the people he had once loved and lost slowly faded away, the bright light disappeared, replaced by beams of light that poured over his face. An unfamiliar male voice spoke next to his ear. Stern, full of power. *God, is that you?* He listened. Waited. The voice told him to breathe, so he did. He felt the water burst from his lungs into his mouth before he spat it out. Firm hands turned him onto his side and he found himself staring into the ground while his lungs expelled more water. A minty smell filled his nostrils. Against the bright yellow rays of the sun, he saw him. It was the stranger, bending down over him. He instantly knew who it was. Sudden fear ripped through his insides. Then confusion set in. *He saved me.* He tried to see his face, but couldn't. Adam drew in a few breaths as his mind slowly separated reality from fantasy. Then suddenly he couldn't feel the man's hands on his back anymore. He looked up to find him but instead looked full into the glorious sunrise he had come there to see.

With his arms extending beneath his body, he pushed himself up into a seated position and stared out at the sunrise, his mind a swirling mess of confusion, his body overflowing with emotions. And as he tried to make sense of it all, the sun flooding his face as it so often did when he used to meet with God, he turned to the one whose knowledge and wisdom would provide all the answers. There, in quiet solitude, as the morning broke, Adam prayed for the first time since the fire. He told God of his innermost fears. He told him how he missed Ruth and Abigail. Thanked him for allowing him to see them one more time, happy and full of heavenly joy. He begged God to forgive him. Asked him to shine a light unto his feet. Surrendered to his will and plan.

THAT SUNDAY ADAM LED HIS FIRST CHURCH GATHERING since the tragedy. He spoke of Christ's grace, and how it comes when one is broken and had nothing to offer in return. And how God gladly takes everyone's sin, their suffering, their brokenness, and gives them new life as his children. He spoke of believers' privilege to serve as agents of grace and how Christ's grace was sufficient for all, ending with the very scripture from Corinthians he had heard that day outside the morgue. *My grace is sufficient for you.*

The church, crammed to the rafters with the last of Turtle Cove's holidaymakers before they would pack up and return home, clung in reverent silence to every word he spoke.

Elsbeth and Daniel smiled from the front pew as they watched. It was what they thought to be one of his best sermons ever. Daniel had noticed that something in

Adam's soul had changed on the last day of their fishing trip. But he knew not to question him about it. It was between him and God. All that mattered was that he had met with God.

When the churchgoers gathered afterward for their End of Summer Celebration, they watched as Adam bid each one farewell.

"I think our boy's going to be just fine. You did good, Daniel. That fishing trip did him the world of good," Elsbeth commented where they stood watching him from a distance.

"We can praise the Almighty for that. All I had to do was get him there."

"Now if only we can do the same for you." He glanced at her sideways. He had noticed she'd been very distant since they got back.

She shuffled uncomfortably, crossing her bony arms as if to close herself off from his inquiring gaze.

"What do you mean? I'm fine."

"No you're not, Beth, and you know it. Out with it. What happened while we were gone?"

"Nothing. Nothing happened. Everything is fine. We spent most of the time gardening or having coffee. Did I tell you that Luke got a new cake supplier and his three-tier chocolate cake is to die for? I was going to order our usual slice of lemon meringue pie, but when I saw that cake I simply couldn't resist."

She was deflecting, and she knew Daniel wouldn't

be fooled, but she had no choice. She didn't want to be trapped in a lie. He wouldn't understand anyway. It was her past and she'd have to deal with it as she had done for the last twenty years and more. It would sort itself out. For now, her secret was safe with Jim, and even if the chief's suspicions about the cause of the fire were made known, Jim still wouldn't tell anyone.

Daniel turned to face her, hands on his broad hips; his eyes squinting with suspicion as he peered into the depths of her soul.

"Hmm, is that right?"

Elsbeth's heart skipped three beats but she held firm her poker face until he spoke again.

"I'll have to go grab me a slice then. Who knows? It might melt away all my worries."

There was no mistaking the look on Daniel's face or that accepting the chocolate cake decoy meant he was tricked into believing she was fine. Deep down he knew Elsbeth was hiding something, but he also knew that sooner or later it would come out. And when it did, he'd be there for her just as he had always been.

"Am I interrupting something?" Adam's voice sounded behind them.

Deciding to let Elsbeth off the hook, Daniel quickly answered.

"We were just saying how proud we are of you. That was quite a message you're sending these people home with," he said.

"I agree! That was incredible, Adam. It's great to have you back," Elsbeth added, grateful that he had interrupted them.

"Just declaring the work of the Lord," Adam replied humbly.

Daniel rested his big hands on Adam's shoulders, like a father would when he expressed pride to his son.

"And a fine job you're doing. Now, you never did tell me how you got that nasty bump on your head. I'm wondering if it might have had something to do with today's preach," Daniel stated as he let go of Adam's shoulders.

Adam cocked his head to one side.

"Let's just say I saw the light. Speaking of which, there's actually something I wanted to ask you both. Something a little more pressing."

"Sounds intriguing. What is it?" Elsbeth asked.

Adam pulled a leaf from the overhanging branch where they stood under a tree and nervously twisted it between his fingers.

"Go on then? What is it?" Daniel pushed.

"Well, the two of you have been there for me since the very first day I came to live here on the island. You are like parents to me and you've been great. But you have never told me about my parents and I have never really asked you how it all happened."

"Well, there was the accident, dear, you know that," Elsbeth said with concern.

"See, that's just it, Elsbeth. I know there was a car accident and that both my parents died, but that's all. I can't remember it. I can't recall anything that happened that day, except maybe my mother's eyes. I can't even remember where we were when the accident happened. And I should. I was twelve. I was old enough to remember. Something, anything, but I can't. There's nothing. How did the accident happen? Were we on holiday? How did I end up staying here?"

Agitated by the haunting questions in his head, Adam tossed the mangled leaf to the ground before plucking a fresh one from the branch and doing the same.

"Where are all these questions coming from, Adam? Why now?" Daniel asked looking troubled.

"I don't know. Maybe it got stirred up with what happened to Ruth and Abigail. All I know is that I can't remember anything and I want to remember. I need to remember. I have to know what happened and how I came to live here at The Lighthouse. What happened to my parents? Who were they?"

The torment in Adam's voice was evident. It was as if his forgotten past, his very existence and purpose had forced its way to the surface without warning. He hadn't been able to stop thinking about it since the morning he almost drowned. Since he had heard his mother's voice telling him to find *it*. Since the stranger had saved his life.

Daniel took a deep breath and held it there for what seemed like forever before he finally spoke again.

"I wish I had all the answers for you, Adam. But the truth is we don't really know. We never could find any concrete answers back then. And we tried. The Lord knows we tried. Eventually, we gave up looking and just accepted God's will for you. Elsbeth, Jim and me were here the day they dropped you off. Everything else remains a mystery to this day."

"Who? Who dropped me off?"

"Two men who said they were from up north, Maryland, if I recall," Elsbeth added. "They must have been your parents' attorneys or something. They had papers, their will, stating that in the event of their simultaneous death you were to come here, under our foster care program. All they said was that you were with your parents and that they had died in a car crash that somehow you survived. As for who your parents were; I guess you should ask your uncle Ben."

Adam stuck his hands inside his pockets and dropped his chin to his chest. His insides felt as if they were slowly being squeezed and twisted; his mind as confused as it was after his heavenly visit. Somewhere deep inside the chambers of his heart there had erupted a yearning that burned like a furnace stoked.

And it wasn't going to be quenched until he found the truth. Or *it*.

CHAPTER TEN

The Internet café was empty when Elsbeth settled into a cubicle in the furthest corner of the cozy shop. She had hoped her plan would pay off since the holidaymakers had all but disappeared and the schools had just reopened. She had stood outside the second-hand bookshop across the street, pretending to look through the books until Roxanne took her usual one p.m. lunch break. As the owner of the café, she had made it a habit to lean in over her customers' shoulders, excusing her watchful eye, as she called it, as being for security reasons. But the entire island knew her nosiness was because Roxanne Dixon liked knowing everyone's business. Which was precisely what she'd blabber out to anyone who'd listen over her daily lunch engagements at Sandals Bistro. And when the town's folk, in turn, needed free publicity or reciprocated with gossip, they trusted her to execute the job well. Elsbeth knew Roxanne was to be avoided at all costs if she'd have any chance of her activity staying secret in Turtle Cove.

Her college dropout son, on the other hand, was the complete opposite. Oliver was tall, withdrawn and permanently stuck behind his mobile phone. One could sneak an elephant past him without him ever looking up. The only reason he stood in for his mother during her lunch breaks and on the weekends was because she paid him handsomely. This was something that irked her no end, but she had somehow convinced herself that it would keep him off the streets and out of trouble. The town, on the other hand, knew full well she had ulterior motives, and that it was a price she was more than willing to pay in exchange for a daily chance at sixty minutes of hot gossip.

ELSBETH'S LEFT LEG BOUNCED NERVOUSLY OFF THE BALL of her foot underneath the table. She had been fretting over whether to go there all week, finally deciding, after another restless night without sleep, that she had no choice. She'd be in and out in twenty minutes. She needed to know where he was. If she was safe. Knowing his whereabouts was the only way she'd have peace. But unexpectedly the rationalization instantly delivered a rush of guilt over taking it in her own strength instead of trusting God for his protection.

She paused her fingers over the computer's keys, chewing hard at her bottom lip as she reconsidered. Her stomach muscles were taut, causing her to feel queasy and suddenly hot and uncomfortable. Just this once, she quickly told herself again. She squeezed her eyelids tightly and took a deep breath before she gave her fingers permission to type his name into the search engine. Her hands were trembling. It had been a long time since she had tried to track his whereabouts except this time she knew it would be much easier. She had glimpsed a headline in one of the newspapers not so long ago that he had since achieved senatorship. His name was bound to pop up in the search.

Her heart pounded in her throat. The very thought of recalling his name, seeing his face again repulsed her. Her little finger hit the *enter* key and in a moment of panic, she shut her eyes again. *It's not too late. You can get up and walk away.* But she knew deep down she couldn't. Or maybe she didn't want to.

When she finally opened her eyes she found herself greeted by a head-and-shoulders image of him grinning from ear to ear. His blond hair had turned ever so slightly white at the temples, and age had settled into his face, but his eyes were still exactly the same. Cold, heartless, capable of anything. A sudden impulse to expel her stomach's contents threatened to push past her uvula at the back of her tongue, causing her to swallow hard before she quickly reached for a mint in her purse.

Sucking hard and fast on the mint she pointed the tiny black computer cursor between his eyes, staring at it for a few seconds. In the past, there had been many occasions where her sinful thoughts had taken hold of her and she had imagined killing him in his sleep in the very spot between his eyes. She had even gone as far as buying a gun. But she could never bring herself to do it. She'd rather die than become like him. Now, too much in her life had changed. Her heart had changed, her very soul. Yet, seeing his face again, suddenly feeling all the familiar emotions she had once felt all those years ago, she knew she had still not forgiven him. Or herself.

She pressed her index finger down onto the computer mouse to access the linked content and scrolled down the page in search of anything that would announce his current location. Nothing. She opened a Washington newspaper's social media account and paused over the highlighted link that had her heart suddenly plunge into her stomach. It read: *Senator Kyle Rudd speaks to supporters in a private campaign rally on the East Coast.*

The shocking news link sent Elsbeth's body into rigor for what seemed to be one of the longest moments of her life. Frozen to the spot, her eyes moved through the text before it hovered back over the date. It coincided with the very week she was certain she had heard footsteps on her porch. It hadn't been her imagination. He *was* there, on her porch. Her mind raced with questions but one lodged in her mind. How had he found her? She had been so careful. He's a senator, Elsbeth! He has the police at his beck and call, she heard her inner voice echo back. Yes, Kyle Rudd's power had extended far beyond the force of his beastly hands and cursing tongue.

Her eyes scanned through the news feed, hoping, praying for something that told her he had left and gone back home. But there was nothing. Angst welled up from the pit of her stomach as she clicked through several more online pages. Fervently probing, hunting him down. But her searches turned up empty.

She recalled seeing a man who looked exactly like him at the town fair and how, at that moment, even though she was convinced it was him, she had brushed it off as nothing but fear playing tricks with her mind. Now she wasn't so sure. All the evidence pointed to the possibility that he was there, lurking in Turtle Cove, looking to take back what he owned. Her throat felt dry and her chest suddenly tight. She had to get out of there. She hurriedly closed down the search pages, grabbed her purse and rushed to the front of the shop where Oliver still sat with his nose in his phone. With her head held down, she slapped some money on the counter and bolted toward the door. Fear had escalated into panic as she now hurriedly made her way back to her car along the sidewalk, not daring to look up once. If he was in town he could be in any of the nearby shops and there was a great chance he would see her. Her feet hit the pavement with force as she increased her pace. Annoyed with herself for intentionally parking her car so far away from the café, she kept her head tucked in and her eyes firmly focused on her feet. Please, Lord, don't let him see me, she prayed.

With tears threatening to run down her cheeks and her insides knotted up, she finally spotted her car on the other side of the busy street. Relieved, she fumbled for the keys inside her bag, never once stopping or looking up. The shrill noise from an oncoming car's horn tried to warn her of its approach, but it was too late. The front of the car thrust into Elsbeth's leg and threw her to the asphalt. Her body bounced off the hard surface before the momentum rolled her to the other side of the road where she came to a jarring halt against the concrete curb. She lay face down like a scattered autumn leaf, one half of her body on top of the gutter, the other draped across the sidewalk. Every fiber in her body ached. One by one her mind processed each passing second until clarity finally presented itself again. Get up, her brain commanded her limbs and she pushed her palms down onto the filthy metal grid and eventually rolled over onto the sidewalk.

"Are you okay? You shouldn't get up." A young woman's voice shrieked next to her.

"I'm fine."

Elsbeth knew full well she wasn't fine when she rose

to her feet and had to lean against a nearby lamppost to stay upright.

"You don't look fine, lady. I should take you to the emergency room. Let me take you," the girl insisted, sounding somewhat panicked.

"No, I'm fine. I just need to get to my car."

"You're crazy! You are in no condition to drive anywhere. As it is my parents are going to kill me for stealing their car. I'm calling an ambulance."

Elsbeth watched as the barely twenty-year-old girl rushed back to find her phone in the car where she had left it in the middle of the road. The accident had caught the attention of several people who had now flocked from the shops and onto the sidewalks. She needed to get out of there and fast. Every moment that passed presented a greater chance of him finding her.

The shocking thought pushed her limbs into motion and Elsbeth dragged herself off to her car, gathering her bag and the few loose items that had slipped out along the way. When she finally reached her car she quickly slipped in behind the wheel and locked the doors. Her hip hurt and she felt dizzy as her fingers fumbled with the key in the ignition. In the distance, she heard the ambulance sirens approaching. With the engine running she quickly flattened the accelerator, turning in front of an approaching car. The vehicle's tires screeched behind her and she glanced at her rearview mirror.

His cold, threatening eyes stared back at her from

behind his steering wheel, sending an icy chill down her spine and into her toes. There was no mistaking it this time. She'd recognize that look anywhere.

With every cell in her body on high alert, Elsbeth let out a panicked scream. She tore her eyes away from his icy stare and pinned it on the road instead. She pushed the vehicle faster along the road that led out of town, praying he hadn't recognized her. Tears poured down her pale cheeks as she wrapped her bony hands around the steering wheel. *This can't be happening! Father, help me get away!* She didn't stop. Didn't once take her foot off the pedal. And she didn't dare look back.

When her car finally approached the last bend before she'd have to turn down toward The Lighthouse, Elsbeth wiped her eyes and nose with the back of her hand and briefly scanned the rearview mirror. Behind her, the road lay stretched out with no cars in sight. She wiped her eyes again, this time turning in her seat to look back so she could be certain he hadn't followed her.

Relief washed over her as she realized she had somehow managed to get away. Perhaps he hadn't recognized her, she didn't know. But what she did know without a doubt is that God had kept his promise to never forsake her. He had helped her escape him once again.

CHAPTER ELEVEN

J im was raking leaves underneath the large oak when Elsbeth's car screeched to a grinding halt in the distance. From where he stood he could see the dusty clouds of smoke kick up in the small parking area behind the first row of cabins. He leaned the rake up against the thick tree trunk and set off toward her. Since the fire incident and the recent stern warning from the fire chief to be extra cautious until the case was resolved, he had cast an extra watchful eye on their community.

As he approached Elsbeth where she had already started heading up the garden path to her cabin he instantly noticed her frazzled demeanor. She had almost killed him by mistaking him for an intruder and he'd let her off the hook without a proper explanation, but everything in him shouted she was in some kind of serious trouble.

"Elsbeth, what's wrong?"

She stormed past him, eager to lock herself in her cabin and never come out again.

"Beth, stop! What's going on? Why are you so upset?"

Still she didn't answer. Her eyes and cheeks were wet from a set of fresh tears and her skin pale and drawn. He rushed after her, shuffling his feet while lifting his shoulders up to his ears to help his aged body keep the pace. She didn't let up, racing down the path as if chased by an unseen predator.

When Jim finally caught up to her, she was fumbling with the key in her door, now crying uncontrollably. Standing behind her, he placed his large callused hands on her shoulders.

"It's okay, Beth. Whatever you're running from, you're safe now," he tried to console her.

"No, I'm not, Jim! He found me! I can't believe he found me."

Elsbeth was a frightened, emotional mess when Jim took the key from her hand and unlocked the door. Once inside, she dashed from window to window, checking each one was properly shut before drawing the drapes.

"What's going on, Beth? Who are you hiding from?"

She ignored him, dashing back to the front door to slip the bolt on the door.

"Beth, stop! I can't help you if you don't tell me what you're so afraid of."

Jim was usually a patient man, but seeing one of his dearest friends fearing for her life drove him crazy.

"He found me, Jim."

"Who?"

"Kyle."

"And who's that?"

She paused, wiping the tears off her jaw, her face suddenly scarlet with shame. It was a part of her life she had gone to great lengths to keep buried for more than twenty years and she had never told a single soul at the mission, ever.

"My husband," she finally whispered, dropping her face into her palms.

Jim fell silent then took a seat at the small dining table. He popped his seagrass fedora upside down on the table in front of him before wiping the fine beads of sweat on his forehead with a red paisley print handkerchief. Still paused near the front door, Elsbeth stood in silence, waiting for him to respond. But he just sat there staring at his hat on the table.

"It happened a very long time ago, Jim. I was young and stupid." She slowly moved across the floor and took a seat opposite him.

"You're married."

She nodded.

"And you ran away from him."

"Yes."

"Why?"

"He hurt me."

"Hurt you how? An affair?"

She shook her head, ashamed to voice it.

"He abused you, physically."

She nodded, dropping her hands in her lap, subconsciously letting it brush over her tummy.

"He's here, Jim. He found me." Elsbeth rose to her feet and moved toward the kettle in the kitchen.

"How do you know? Did you see him?"

"Yes, in town. And in the newspapers."

Her last statement piqued Jim's interest.

"What do you mean? He's wanted by the police?"

"I wish, but no. He's well, famous of sorts." She nervously poured hot water into two mugs as she waited for Jim to connect the dots.

And it didn't take him long to do so.

"Oh, please tell me it's not Kyle Rudd, the politician."

The look on her face confirmed it, and Jim shot to his feet and started pacing the small space.

"Let me get this straight. You're married to Senator Kyle Rudd who you ran away from over twenty years ago. Because he abused you. And you came here, to Turtle Cove to get away from him."

"I know, I know! It's insane but it's all true, Jim. He's not the exemplary man everyone thinks he is."

Jim scooped his coffee cup from the counter and took his seat again at the table. After he took two big mouthfuls of coffee he sat back and looked her full in the eye.

"If this man is dangerous you need to tell me everything, Beth."

She nodded, knowing there was no turning back now. She trusted Jim with her life and she was in over her head. The man she feared most in life was capable of anything to get what he wanted and she couldn't risk the mission and the lives of everyone who had become her family. There was no telling what he would do to get to her. She wrapped her hands around her coffee mug as she sat down at the table, drawing a deep breath before she spoke again.

"I met him during a small peaceful protest in our local town when I was just twenty-four. He was in his final year studying law and before I knew it we were married the instant he graduated. The first few years were great. He worked at a small law firm in Maryland. Life was good. We dreamed of having a family and tried for three years to fall pregnant, but never did. During that time he was introduced into politics but the constituents demanded he resembled the family man he portrayed in his campaigns. And since we didn't have children he blamed me for tarnishing his image, accusing me of sabotaging his career. That's when everything changed, almost overnight. He started working late, went away on business trips, spent more and more time at the office. I kept trying to get pregnant but nothing worked. Then one day I suggested he got himself checked out since the doctors had already told me there was no reason for me not to fall pregnant. He lost it. That was the first time he hit me, right across the face. A week later it happened again, and again. I couldn't stop him. To the world, we looked like the perfect couple, but behind closed doors, he was a monster who blamed me for everything that went wrong in his life. I stuck it out for years, covering my bruises with make-up, hiding behind sunglasses. I kept thinking it would all change when I fell pregnant or he got elected, whichever came first. I forgave him, over and over. Until the day he shattered my arm in three places. I had to lie to the doctor, said I slipped and fell on a freshly mopped floor. A week later I found out I was pregnant. That was the day I decided to leave him. There was no way I'd let him hurt my child. So I waited until he left for another business trip, took whatever cash I had managed to skim off the grocery budget, and got on the next bus out of town. I had planned to go to Florida to stay with my mother, but she suddenly fell ill and soon after passed. I had nowhere to go, no money, and was almost ten weeks pregnant. I had no choice but to go back and tell him about the baby in the hopes it would change him."

Elsbeth paused, wiping a lonely tear that had slipped down onto her cheek before she continued.

"When I got home he was waiting for me. He'd been drinking. I had never seen him angrier. He was livid that I tried to leave him. I lied and told him I was just visiting with my mother, but he didn't believe me. I never even got a chance to tell him about the baby. He lost all control. I couldn't stop him. He threw me against the wall and kicked me until I finally passed out. When I woke up the next morning he had left on another trip. Two days later I lost the baby, right there in the bathroom. So I buried my unborn child in the garden near the lavender bush and left. This time I colored my hair and changed my name. Somehow I found my way here and never left."

Jim sat in shocked silence as she finished telling him her story. His heart ached for her. Suddenly he knew exactly how Elsbeth Porter had become the strong woman of faith they had all come to depend on. She had been molded, hammered out by life's cruel hands, and brought to Turtle Cove to be restored by her Savior's grace.

He leaned across the table and took hold of both her hands.

"No woman should ever go through what you did. You were incredibly brave to leave him."

"I don't think I was brave. I was a coward. I should

have told him I was pregnant. Maybe then the baby would have had a chance at life."

"Is that what you think? You're harboring guilt over something you had no control over. A man who disrespected you."

"I killed my baby, Jim. If I had told him before I left the first time, things could have been different. He would have had the child he so desperately needed to save his career. It was all my fault."

"Beth, the man is a monster. *He* kicked you to a pulp, not you. Even if you had told him you were pregnant, there's no way of knowing what he would have done to both of you. You did the right thing to protect your unborn child and yourself. You got away."

Elsbeth moved to clean the empty coffee mugs in the kitchen sink. She acknowledged what Jim said made all the sense in the world; yet, she didn't believe any of it. If she hadn't tried to leave him, hadn't angered him, her baby would have never died. She had vowed to protect her baby at all costs, and she had failed miserably. The one opportunity she had to be the mother she always wanted to be, she had recklessly thrown away.

Her mind trailed to Adam and how she had taken him in as if he were her own child. She loved him with a mother's heart and was grateful to have had at least that. He was her gracious gift from God.

"Adam! Where's Adam?" She suddenly spun around, startling Jim with her panicked question.

"Kyle is here, in Turtle Cove, Jim, and I am positive he was here on my porch that night. What if he somehow found out about the baby and now wants to take his revenge on me by hurting Adam? He is capable of anything, Jim. I won't let him hurt Adam. I won't let him take him away from me too!"

Jim was next to her, then held her tight.

"For as long as I have breath in my body, Beth, that man will not come near you or hurt anyone here at the mission or in Turtle Cove. Least of all Adam."

But Elsbeth wasn't so sure. No one knew Kyle the way she did. She had learned that what lay behind his charming veneer, was a dark soul that would stop at nothing to inflict his selfish will. Kyle Rudd was an evil man scorned who would kill her if he had half a chance.

And as quickly as fear penetrated her armor, the words recorded by the psalmist rang in her head.

A thousand may fall at your side, ten thousand at Your right hand, but it will not come near you.

A faint smile lifted at the corners of her thin lips. What Kyle didn't know was that Victoria Rudd was already dead. He had killed her a long time ago. Elsbeth Porter was stronger, a new creation firmly planted in Christ, and she would rise up against evil with the strength of the God who saved her.

CHAPTER TWELVE

W hen Adam crossed the state lines into Florida he couldn't help feeling anxious. In all the years on the island, he had never wanted to learn about his parents. He never asked. He had told himself that it wasn't necessary. It wouldn't change the fact that they were dead. Elsbeth, Daniel, and the rest of the community at the mission had taken him in and they had made him feel loved and safe. That seemed good enough for him. And, as time went on, he remembered less and less of his parents until he no longer remembered them at all. Except for his mother's eyes.

But now he wasn't sure about anything. Perhaps he had intentionally blocked them and the accident from his memory. Moved on. Because knowing, remembering, hurt too much. He had no idea, but what he did know, was what he saw that day in the creek. It wasn't a dream. He believed that with all his heart. And something deep inside his spirit told him to follow his heart. Where his search would lead him, he didn't quite know. But he had asked the Lord to guide him and trusted that he would.

He took another bite of the chicken sandwich Elsbeth had packed for him and wiped the mayonnaise that had dribbled down his chin. He'd wanted to fly to Tampa, but Elsbeth and Jim had insisted he drove. Both had felt a solitary road trip and getting away from the island for a bit would do him good. It had piqued his curiosity but, since they were both in agreement, and adamant at that, he didn't argue. For all he knew it was the very guidance he had prayed for.

He recalled the telephone conversation he'd had with his uncle the day before. He had intended to discuss the accident over the phone, but something in his uncle's voice had changed. His tone was almost guarded. As if he knew something no one else did and didn't know if he should say. It frustrated Adam. What was his uncle hiding and why? He was his only remaining blood relative as far as he knew, and the one thought that persisted in the back of his mind was why his uncle didn't take him in.

THE REMAINING THREE HOURS WENT BY QUICKLY. Consumed mostly by the lingering thoughts and questions that swirled in his head. By the time he pulled into his uncle's driveway, he was feeling tense and irritated. The front door flew open the moment he turned off the car's engine and a second later his uncle's large frame stood in the doorway. Adam studied his face as he shut the car's door behind him and walked around the car toward him, his overnight bag slung over his shoulder. His uncle looked worn out, almost sad, but hidden beneath the obvious, was clear evidence of nervous tension.

"Hey, Uncle Ben," Adam greeted.

"It's good to see you, Adam."

Ben took his nephew's bag and ushered him inside. Adam could tell he felt uncomfortable. Truth be told, so did he. Ben showed him to one of the bedrooms and set his bag down on the bed.

"It's not much but hopefully it will do," he excused.

The room was tiny and modestly decorated with chocolate brown curtains and a matching bedspread thrown untidily over a single bed that stood squashed in one corner. Against the room's stark turquoise walls it somewhat overwhelmed Adam's senses but he didn't say anything.

"It's perfect, thank you, Uncle Ben."

"I have a pitcher of sweet tea ready in the sitting room. You must be thirsty from the long drive."

He led the way to the open-plan sitting room where Adam sat down on the two-seater sofa. The large pink flowers against the dark military green backdrop with matching fringe yelled 1970s. Yet it looked as good as new. Opposite him, Ben dropped down into the matching green armchair and pushed the footrest out from underneath. Next to him, a newspaper lay folded to the sports page on a small antique side table. Adam allowed his eyes to take in the small house. It was dated but pristine.

"It doesn't look like much, I know. With your aunt in the care home I haven't really bothered with it to be honest. No one ever visits and it's not like she remembers anything after she spends a weekend here. As far as she knows it's still 1974. The doctor said he suspects that's when something triggered the dementia. He says keeping it this way might help jar her memory, but it hasn't really."

He shuffled uncomfortably in his seat then folded his large hands over his round belly. His uncle was never one to mince his words and it didn't take him long to push past the pleasantries and tackle the reason Adam had come.

"I always knew this day would come, you know. But I'll be honest. I kind of hoped it wouldn't," he said.

"I'm sorry."

"What for? You have every right to be asking about your parents. It's something I should have discussed with you a long time ago."

"Why haven't you?"

"Not sure. I figured you'd come to me when the time was right."

He pushed his chin out toward a navy blue with gold trim photo album that lay on the coffee table between them.

"There isn't a lot in there, but it's all I have. Your parents weren't much for taking photos. I never could get either of them to agree to be in any pictures. Your mother wasn't always like that though. It only became a thing once she married your father. Then suddenly she didn't like anyone taking any pictures of them, and especially of you after you were born."

Adam sat forward and flipped the album open. A large portrait of his mother greeted him, her piercing blue eyes staring back at him. She was sitting in a field, chewing on a piece of grass, her hair beautifully done up, her smile big and wide. She looked happy.

"How old was she here?" Adam asked.

"Fresh out of college, if I recall. She wanted to be a teacher."

"I can't remember her ever working."

"She didn't. Not since the day she had you. She always said she didn't want to miss a moment with you. But—"

Ben paused.

"But what, Uncle Ben?"

Ben looked away and then back at Adam.

"It's just my feeling, okay. But I always felt it was

because your father didn't want her to work. He seemed to like her being at home, hidden away from the world."

Adam didn't like the insinuation or tone in his uncle's voice, but he let it go. He flipped to the next page. It was a wedding photo of his parents cutting their cake. His father was dressed in a naval uniform."

"My father was in the navy? I never knew that."

"When they first met, yes. That picture is the only one I have of him. I had sneaked the photo. I thought your mother needed at least one photo of their wedding day."

"So he left the navy then?"

Ben shrugged his shoulders.

"I never knew what work your father did, Adam. No one did. He was, how shall I put it, very to himself."

"What do you mean?"

"Nothing. I'm not sure. All I know is that he didn't want your mother to leave the house, not even to go to the grocer. He did all the shopping. She was allowed to go as far as the bus stop where she'd see you off for school at the naval base and then meet you again afterward. I recall her saying she had a few friends come over for tea once or twice a month, but that was it. Oh, and church on Sundays, but then your father was with her. She never complained about it though. She seemed happy, so I never pushed her about it."

Adam flipped through the album. The pages had mostly pictures of his uncle and his mother as babies and young children, and one picture of his mother as a young teenager.

"Where did you grow up?"

"Ah, right here, in Tampa. Best place in the entire world. We had a great childhood."

"And my father?"

"Not sure. He never said. He met your mother while on vacation here in Tampa. He was stationed at the marine base in Pensacola at the time. They moved there once they got married. You were born there too. In the naval hospital."

Adam fell silent as he digested all the information his uncle had shared.

"Go on then, ask me." His uncle's calm voice came.

"What?"

"What you've been dying to ask me more than anything. Why I didn't take you in after the accident."

Was it that obvious? Adam thought. But his uncle was right. The question had been burning in his mind ever since the fishing trip. His eyes met his uncle's as he waited for the answer.

Ben pushed the footrest back in its place inside his chair and leaned forward, his elbows resting on his knees and his big hands clasped in front of him.

"Your mother called me up one day, just after your twelfth birthday. She called me from a phone booth, which I thought was very strange, but I figured she was hiding it from your father."

"Why?"

"Your father and I, well, we didn't get on too well. I wanted him to loosen the reins on your mother a bit. We argued about that a lot. He told me it wasn't any of my business and your mother, much to my surprise, agreed. So we had a big fallout one year before Christmas. Anyway, I hadn't spoken to her in quite some time after that, until that day she called me. She told me that if anything ever happened, and you survived, I had to make sure you got to The Lighthouse. We used to go there as children. My parents, your grandparents, had volunteered there for many years so we had gone there each summer. In fact, the very cabin you lived in was once our family's cabin. It's where your aunt Agnes and I first met too. Your mother loved you more than anything or anyone in the entire world. And for some reason, she felt you would be better off there. She had me draw up legal papers and everything. I fought her on it for months but she insisted. Said it was the only place you'd be free. I never knew what she meant. I never got the chance to ask her."

Adam got up and walked over to the nearby window that overlooked the small backyard. His heart felt as if it was going to explode with emotion. He had hoped to leave there with all the answers but all this visit was doing was create more questions.

"I know. It's a lot. And I'm sorry for not telling you all this sooner. But once I saw how happy you were on the island, there was no reason to upset you more than you've already had to cope with. I believe God's timing is perfect and for some reason, this now feels like it's exactly the right time."

Adam returned to the sofa.

"What happened that day, Uncle Ben? Where did the accident happen? What happened? I can't remember anything."

This time it was Ben who got up and walked to retrieve a wooden object from inside a hidden compartment behind the bookshelf. When he came back he sat down next to Adam on the sofa and handed it to him.

"I wish I had all the answers but I don't. I believe that this might lead to the answers you need."

CHAPTER THIRTEEN

Elsbeth nervously paced the room at The Lighthouse. It usually served as their prayer room but they had thought it best to use for their meeting with the fire chief today. Although it was small, the meeting didn't involve the entire mission's team so it seemed perfect. They also knew they wouldn't be interrupted.

"You're going to wear a track in these floors if you don't stop, Beth," Daniel commented from where he patiently sat waiting at the nearby table for the chief to arrive.

She ignored him and pushed her forefinger and thumb between the blind's slats to study the mission's main entrance.

"That's the hundredth time you've done that. It's not ten o'clock yet, Beth. What's your hurry anyway?"

She shot a nervous eye at Jim where he quietly sat at

the table next to Daniel. The look in his eyes told her not to say anything just yet.

"Nothing. I just have a few things to take care of afterward."

"You can sit this one out if you like."

Her head spun around at Daniel's suggestion and she was quick to answer.

"No, don't be silly. It's not that urgent. Besides, I am far too curious to know why the chief called this meeting."

"That makes two of us. It's been months since the incident. Might just be to give us suggestions on preventative measures," Danny said. "Speaking of Jim, what's with all the sudden security? The mayor ran late for his meeting the other day because he got stuck this side of that fancy access gate you had installed."

"Yeah, sorry about that. Just a few teething problems, but I've sorted it out. Won't happen again."

"Is it really necessary? I mean, we've been running this mission for almost thirty years and we have never had any security issues. Why now?"

Jim nervously adjusted his hat that lay in front of him on the table.

"Simple. Because it *has* been thirty years. Times have changed and one can never be too careful. We owe it to our guests, the camp kids, and everyone else who comes here to make sure we keep them safe. Who knows who comes through those doors?"

"Well, hopefully, the lost trying to make sense of their broken lives. We don't want to turn anyone away now, do we? I just think you should have put it to the team to discuss and decide on together."

Daniel's tone made it very clear that he was displeased. But, much to Jim's relief, it was at that precise moment that Elsbeth interrupted them.

"He's here!" She started pacing again as she picked at her thumbnail.

"Great! Maybe now you will take a seat and relax a little. I don't know what's gotten into you, Beth," Daniel said as he stepped outside to welcome the chief in.

Using the opportunity, Elsbeth whispered into Jim's ear.

"This is bad, Jim. I know the chief is here to tell us the fire wasn't an accident."

"We don't know that, Beth. Calm down. We'll handle things as they come. Just sit down and keep your wits about you."

"It was Kyle, Jim. I know it. He found me and he wants to get back at me by hurting Adam."

"Elsbeth, you're proposing murder here. Do you know how ridiculous that sounds?"

"Not when Kyle Rudd is involved, trust me!"

While Elsbeth settled into her chair at the table, Daniel and Chief Perry entered the room. Elsbeth's nerves were shot. It didn't matter that Jim didn't agree with her. She knew. Deep down it had suddenly all become crystal clear to her. Kyle was a man who held grudges and he had made it very clear that he would kill her if she ever tried to run away from him again. Well, she had and it had taken twenty years for him to find her, but he had.

"Well, Chief, this doesn't happen too often. You have us all curious over your visit," said Daniel.

"And I'm afraid it's not going to be a pleasant one. We finally concluded our investigation."

The room fell silent as they watched Chief Perry open a folder, spreading the contents across the table in front of them.

"What are we looking at?" Daniel asked as his eyes scanned the half-dozen photos.

"Evidence."

"Of what?"

"Arson."

It was as if Daniel's face had frozen in time. He sat there, mouth open, staring at the chief. Elsbeth, on the other hand, started pacing the room again, arms folded tightly over her chest and her face strained. Behind her, Jim sat in silence. The chief's revelation confirmed what he had already suspected.

"You cannot be serious," Daniel finally said, his voice low and contemplative.

"I'm afraid I am, Danny. We were very thorough and made double certain of our facts. The evidence doesn't lie."

Daniel sat back in his chair as he rubbed one hand over the nearly bald patch on the crown of his head.

"Arson. Someone deliberately set fire to Adam's cabin and murdered his family. And you're absolutely sure."

The chief nodded. "No doubt whatsoever. We don't deal with many cases like these so I had to call in an expert team from Charleston. That's why the investigation took a bit longer than intended."

"How?" Jimmy spoke for the first time. Elsbeth stopped midway behind him to listen.

"Using one of the oldest tricks in the book when it comes to wanting it to appear accidental. The electric iron. These photos here show what was left of the source. Based on our investigation the fire started in the pantry. The iron was left on the top shelf, switched on. We ruled out any possibility of the device malfunctioning. And since neither Ruth nor Adam's height makes them likely to use a shelf that high up, it's highly unlikely to have been negligence on their part. Also, the pantry door was locked and all the air vents blocked except for the two leading to the bedrooms. The perpetrator had every intention of killing them, most probably in their sleep."

Elsbeth's sobs caused Daniel to reach out to console her while he spoke again.

"Chief, I don't understand why anyone would want

to commit such a heinous act. It makes no sense. Who would want to kill Ruth and Abigail?"

"That is now for the police to determine. You are likely to have them come by as soon as this afternoon. But my guess is that it wasn't directed only at Ruth and Abigail."

Daniel's face instantly declared the shockwaves that had bolted through his body.

"You mean whoever did this wanted all three of them dead?"

"I believe so, yes. Which tells me they were amateurs and quite possibly from out of town. Anyone who knows Adam well enough or has visited the island more than once will tell you he's out on his surfboard before the sun even rises. He's been doing it every day since he was, what, thirteen?"

The chief's words left Elsbeth icy cold and now sobbing uncontrollably.

Jim, who had quietly been listening, looked back at Elsbeth. His eyes told her that she should speak up. But he was greeted with nothing but fear in her eyes. It wasn't his story to tell, so he kept quiet.

"I think I'm going to be sick," she suddenly announced as she bolted for the door.

With Elsbeth out of the room, Daniel took his seat at the table again. He leaned close to Jim.

"You knew, didn't you?"

"I had my suspicions but I wasn't sure."

"Why, Jim? Why didn't you come to me? How long have you known?"

"Not long," the chief answered for him. "I thought it best to share my suspicions with Jim. We were still waiting on the final results to come in and didn't want to cause unnecessary panic."

Daniel sat back in his chair, one side of his mouth pulling to the side.

"That's why you had all these fences and gates installed."

Jim nodded.

"I did what I thought was best."

Daniel drew his chest full of air and then blew it out, puffing his cheeks in the process.

"We're going to have to tell Adam."

"I would urge you to, yes. The police are going to want to speak with him. But I reckon it's best he hears about it from you. You might want to keep an eye on him too. By now the entire island knows he survived and there's a good chance whoever did this will come after him again."

"We sent him out of town for a bit. He left early this morning," Jim divulged.

"Elsbeth knew too? Really Jim?"

"And that's my cue, fellows. I'll leave you two to talk it out. If you have any more questions, you know where to find me."

. . .

ELSBETH STARED AT HER IMAGE IN THE MIRROR. SHE had made it to the ladies' bathroom just in time before she emptied the entire contents of her stomach. Her face was gray, her eyes red and swollen from all the crying. She cupped her hands under the tap and splashed the cool water over her face before she looked up at her reflection again. The woman who stared back at her wasn't Elsbeth Porter. It was Victoria Rudd. She was two decades older, and her hair was different. But her eyes were filled with the same fear. The same shame. The same weakness.

"No!" she shouted out then splashed another few handfuls of water over her face before drying her hands on the loose fabric on her hips. She smoothed her hair from her face and adjusted her blouse. When she was satisfied, she straightened her shoulders, pushed out her chin and spoke out loud to her reflection.

"You are Elsbeth Porter. You are NOT that woman anymore. You are a new creation in Christ. You have conquered. You are strong through him who gives you strength. Though you walk through the valley of death, you shall fear no evil. For he has rescued you."

Her words echoed in the empty bathroom but Elsbeth did what she had done every time she felt the enemy's attack for almost two decades since she had come to know Christ. God had brought her to The Lighthouse, her safe haven, and he wasn't about to fail her now.

As peace washed over her she thanked God for saving Adam from the fire. Asked him to have his hand of protection over the son she never birthed. She thanked him for his grace and for taking him away and out of danger.

CHAPTER FOURTEEN

Adam stared at the flat piece of wood in his lap. Roughly the size of a thick novel, it was hand-carved from some kind of dark wood he didn't recognize. There were no hinges or anything to indicate it could be opened. Just an oddly shaped indentation that almost appeared to look as if it was a drawer, and the decorative pattern along its edges that looked like the waves in the ocean on a windy day. It had no keyholes or any other type of lock anywhere.

"What is it?"

"It was your father's. He left it here one night, just days before the accident. It was quite strange actually. He wasn't one to just pop in for an impromptu visit, much less without your mother and in the middle of the night. He woke me up, you know. Incessantly banging on my door at two o'clock in the morning, all dressed in black as if he was some secret spy or something. At first, I thought something had happened to your mother, or you, but then he pushed the piece of wood into my hand, said to keep it safe until the time was right to give it to you and left. I never saw him again."

Adam shook the object next to his ear.

"Is there anything inside?"

"I haven't the foggiest. I have never been able to figure out how to open it or even if it could be opened. There are strange number sequences on the back, in each of the corners, but I haven't figured out what they mean or what to do with them."

Adam flipped the wooden object over and studied the numbers. Each corner had several small numbers engraved into the wood. He ran his fingers over them, then held it up to the light that streamed in through the window behind him to better inspect it.

"They're not dates if that's what you're thinking. I already looked into that. The numbers are too big and the sequence is all wrong."

Adam dropped it onto the table and slumped back into the couch.

"I have no idea what I'm supposed to do with all of this. Nothing makes any sense. I came here for answers and all I have is more questions. Some stranger stalks me but then saves me. I lost my wife and daughter, it's all too much!"

He got up and walked over to the large window

overlooking the back garden, his hands clasped behind his neck. His stomach twisted with confusion. Two seconds later, his uncle stood behind him.

"What man?"

His words had Adam turn to face him, perplexed by the look in his uncle's eyes.

"What man, Adam?" Ben asked again, sounding more urgent than before.

"I don't know. Just a man. I saw him the day of the funeral, then at the town fair, watching me from a distance. I thought he was out to hurt me, but then when I nearly drowned on a fishing trip the other day, he saved me. I'd be dead if it weren't for him."

Ben swung around and took the three strides into the kitchen, knocking his walking stick to the floor in his haste. Adam watched as he yanked one of the drawers open and tipped all of its contents over onto the floor before placing it upside down onto the kitchen island that now separated them. Stuck to the bottom of the drawer was an old brown letter-sized envelope which he plucked off and pulled out a newspaper clipping, his clumsy fingers fumbling to unfold it.

"Is this the guy?" He slid the piece of paper across the counter, his fat index finger thumping down on it.

Adam took in the details of the black and white newspaper clipping. Big bold letters read *Miracle Boy Escapes Fatal Car Crash.* Below it, an image of a light-colored car, wrecked beyond recognition, sat wedged and suspended between two large trees. And there, behind one of the trees in the background, was the unmistakable frame of the stranger.

It was as if a bolt of lightning had just struck Adam's body. Unable to speak he stared at the picture. The stranger was younger in the photo but there was no mistaking him.

"I knew it! That's him, isn't it?" Ben yelled as he made his way back around the kitchen island and scooped up his walking stick before he marched off to the sitting room and slumped back down in his chair. When Adam finally took his seat on the sofa opposite him, the article still in his hand, his eyes met his uncle's.

"You know who this is?" he asked.

Ben briefly paused before he answered.

"Yes, no, not exactly."

He scooped forward and poured himself another glass of sweet tea and gulped it down in less than three seconds.

Adam waited for him to speak, his eyes urging his uncle to do so.

"What I mean is that I have seen him before, yes, but I don't know his name or exactly who he is. When I saw this photo in the paper the day after the accident I got suspicious. Look at him. He's just standing there, staring at everything, black trench coat in the middle of the summer and all. That's creepy if ever you've seen it. So I paid the reporter a visit. He didn't know who the man was; never even saw him at the scene. He told me to leave it to him to investigate. The next thing I know he ends up dead under the Miami pier. They ruled it an accident, but I've always thought otherwise. All his notes, every single photograph he took that day, all of it, gone! Vanished into thin air! I tried for years to find this man. One time I was sure I saw him over there, under the streetlight in the middle of the night. Just standing there. But when I went out to see, he was gone. It's like my mind was playing tricks on me or something. You think you see something but then in a blink of an eye it's gone."

"I know what you mean," Adam said under his breath.

His eyes skimmed through the words in the article. Several words caught his attention. *Mystery couple, possible naval interference, not an accident.* Adam couldn't read any more. He tossed the paper onto the coffee table and took up his stance at his spot by the glass door that overlooked the garden. Suddenly his throat tightened and he found it hard to breathe. In a hurried attempt to get outside for fresh air his fingers clumsily fumbled the patio door's lock. Seconds later he undid the latch and slipped the door open before stumbling out onto the small patio. Bent over at the waist, gasping for air, he fell to his knees and sought answers from God.

When Adam finally fell asleep much later that night, flashing images from deep within his subconscious disturbed his sleep. He was in the backseat of a car with his head rested against the doorframe of a Beetle that somehow he knew had once belonged to his grandfather. He was in the body of a young boy, around twelve. His eyes traced the white clouds that rapidly changed shape against their bright blue backdrop through the car window. The sun caressed his cheeks and the warm ocean breeze pushed through the open car windows and gently swept his hair from his eyes. He smiled. He was happy. He turned his eyes to the seats in front of him and saw his parents. His father was driving, his mother in the passenger seat in front of him. They looked happy too. He's wishing that they could stay like that forever. Then suddenly he is flying high above a beat-up mint green 1960s VW that's making its way along a coastal road to where the road eventually snaked between the trees of a lush forest. And as quickly as he soared above the car he was suddenly transported back into the backseat. His eyes were fixed on the tall trees that seemed to pierce holes in the now cloudless sky. In the stillness of his mind, he strung the trees in sequential bundles that made no sense at all. Counting them in a solitary game he played on repeat. He sees the kids at school, making fun of him. They call him out saying he's weird. He's alone. His mother's voice cuts through the torture and tells him that he is extra special and made perfect in Christ. Then he is back in the moving car between the trees, lost somewhere in their repetitive patterns when a sudden thud came from somewhere behind them. It jerked the car forward and nearly threw him off his seat. His father's deep voice yells for him to get down behind their seats. So he does, moments before there is another hard hit against their car from behind. He's scared, crouching down behind the front seats. He sees his mother's piercing blue eyes looking at him over her backrest, then, without warning he feels his body lifting off the floorboard to where it floats in the cavity between the car's roof and the seats as if they were traveling through the air between the towering trees. Then everything went quiet around him and he was alone. He shouted for his mother, then his father, but neither answered. He couldn't move. He couldn't see them. He yelled for them again. Over and over but still they didn't answer.

"Adam! Wake up!"

The sound of Ben's voice ripped through his mind and jerked him away from the trees. He ignored it. He tried to call his mom again, but his uncle's voice interfered. Then suddenly he was sitting upright in someone's bed.

"Adam, it's me, Uncle Ben. You okay, man? You

were shouting so loud you almost blew off the roof on my house."

Adam took in his surroundings. The turquoise walls and chocolate curtains told him where he was.

"There we go. I'll get you some water. You must have had a nightmare or something. You gave me the fright of my life there for a minute."

Adam watched as Ben waddled out of his bedroom and down the passage to the kitchen.

It wasn't a nightmare, and he knew it. He stared at the newspaper clipping that lay next to the night lamp beside the bed. His eyes settled on the wreckage. The picture was black and white so there was no telling what color the car was, much less the make. In his dream, he saw the car, clear as day. A dusty mint green, vintage VW Beetle with tan seats.

Ben returned in a hurry, spilling water as he came toward him.

"Drink up. I added a few spoons of sugar to help you settle down. Care to tell me what all that was about?" Ben said as he sat back down on the bed.

Adam gulped the liquid down before he spoke.

"What make was the car? What color was it?"

A fine line across his uncle's brow marked his curiosity at his sudden question.

"Which car?"

"My parents' car. The one from the accident."

"Ah, yes. It was a Beetle, your grandfather's actually. Light green with tan leather seats. I can still smell the leather. I used to love that car. Why?"

"I think I just recalled the accident, Uncle Ben. In more detail than I care to remember."

"You did, did you? I figured your mind had blocked it but that's great, Adam. It's been twenty years since it happened and you have never been able to recall anything, ever. "

"I wish I hadn't."

"Tell me what you remember."

"I remember everything. And—" he paused and dropped his head back while he closed his eyes.

"It wasn't an accident. Someone drove us off the road. Someone who had every intention of killing us all. Uncle Ben, my parents were murdered."

CHAPTER FIFTEEN

"You don't seem the slightest bit surprised," Adam said when his uncle's face revealed as much.

He watched as Ben got to his feet and left the bedroom without saying a word. Jumping from the bed, he quickly followed his uncle down the short passage and into the kitchen.

"Uncle Ben, what are you not telling me? Why aren't you surprised by what I said?"

But his uncle didn't utter a single word. He simply busied himself with a couple of coffee mugs and proceeded to run water into the kettle. Adam didn't push the issue, but he had the sinking feeling his uncle knew far more than he had told him. From the corner of the poorly lit kitchen, he stood in silence as he watched Ben prepare two cups of coffee. He waited for him to say something with patience he knew was not his own. But

Ben didn't speak. His mind was elsewhere. It was just shy of four a.m. when they each took a seat at the round oak dining table just off the kitchen. And in a low monotone voice, while staring into his steaming mug of coffee, Ben finally spoke.

"Adam, I understand all this information is probably a lot to bear. And it makes sense that, after the trauma of losing your wife and child it might have taken its toll on your emotional and psychological state, but you can't let it mess with your head. I am deeply sorry you lost both your parents and your family, truly I am, but you need to keep your wits about you, son. You should let sleeping dogs lie."

Adam sat in stunned silence. This was not what he had expected to hear. His uncle's hollow words ran through his head and finally stopped in the pit of his stomach. *Let sleeping dogs lie. What does that mean?* He needed to know what his gut relentlessly screamed at him.

"I'm not going to let it go, Uncle Ben. You know I just remembered everything. It wasn't a nightmare. I recalled the accident. I felt them push the car off the side of the road. I heard my father yell at me to take cover. Why? He looked scared. He sounded scared. So were my mother's eyes. This wasn't a dream. How could it have been if I didn't have any of the car's details? This was very real, and you know it. Why won't you tell me what you know?"

"What difference will it make, huh? They're dead. It won't bring them back, Adam. It's been twenty years, son."

Ben's voice sounded agitated.

"I can't let it go, Uncle Ben. I need to know the truth. Someone killed my parents, and that stranger is somehow involved. And you know it too. You already knew it back then when you asked the reporter to look into it. The same people who killed my parents probably killed him too. Why?"

Ben grunted from behind the lip of the coffee mug and took a large mouthful of coffee.

"You need to help me find the stranger, Uncle Ben. Figure out what this block of wood is and why my father left it for me. This is all I have left of them."

He watched his uncle contemplate his request and prayed God would stir his heart to help him. He needed to know the truth. He believed with all his heart that God had brought him there to find the truth. At that moment he knew beyond a shadow of a doubt that it was what he was meant to do.

Ben lowered his mug to the table and looked up to meet his nephew's pleading eyes.

"You sure you want to do this?"

Adam nodded in silence.

"Things could get dangerous, Adam. We might be in over our heads. That reporter didn't lose his life over nothing. Are you prepared for that?"

"Without a doubt."

"If, and I repeat, IF there was someone out there who did kill your parents, and *possibly* the reporter, then they won't hesitate to kill you too."

"I have nothing left to lose, Uncle Ben."

"You have the mission, son. God's work."

"Daniel and the team will carry the mission forward. They are more than competent. I trust that God brought me here, to this precise moment, Uncle Ben, and I know what I know. This is what he wants me to do. I am meant to find the truth, wherever that might lead me."

Ben's mouth suddenly curled at the corners.

"You're exactly like your mother, you know that? I never could convince her of anything. Once she got it in her head to do something, there was no stopping her."

He gathered the empty mugs in one hand and took them through to the kitchen, shouting back over his shoulder.

"I suggest we get dressed then. We have a long day ahead of us."

WHEN ADAM SETTLED INTO THE PASSENGER SEAT OF HIS uncle's car his heart was thumping against his chest. He was anxious, yes, but more than that, there was an exhilarating feeling of anticipation that bubbled through his veins. He had barely any memory of his parents at all but somehow it felt as if he was about to go meet them for the very first time. His fingers nervously clutched the wooden item in his lap. His father had left him this gift, a gift wrapped up in danger and mystery. And while he couldn't deny that it made him fearful to head off into the unknown, he knew with all his heart that he was ready for whatever came his way.

"Where are we going?" he asked his uncle as they drove off.

"To the crash site. I thought we should start there. Maybe it will trigger a memory of some sort. Your aunt's doctors have me do it with her all the time. We drive around to all the places we once spent time together. The ice cream truck by the pier, the library where she used to love spending time, even her hair salon."

"And has it worked?"

"Not really. Sometimes she remembers small things but it never really sticks or leads to any bigger memories that have any significance."

"Was she close to my parents?"

"She got along with your father much better than me. Probably because she loved your mother like a sister. She never had any siblings. It was your mother who introduced Agnes to me, actually. They had been friends for a long time. They often had tea together or went shopping, before your father kept her all to himself."

Adam shuffled uncomfortably in his seat in response to his uncle's words.

"Sorry, son, I shouldn't have said that. I just feel like he robbed us of spending valuable time with my sister. We used to be the best of friends before they got married. I guess I have never really forgiven him for that."

"I get it. I lost my mother and you lost your sister. We're both carrying our own hurt. I believe God has mercy for that."

They both sat in silence for the rest of the short drive heading south out of Tampa.

"Didn't you say we lived in Pensacola?"

"Yup, you did."

"Then why are we heading south?"

"That, my dear nephew, is a question that has haunted me for the last twenty years. At first, I thought you all had left to go on a trip, maybe down to Venice Beach. Your mother always loved it there. But there was no luggage in the car, not even your toothbrushes."

"Well, we just passed the turnoff to Venice."

"Precisely. Keep your eyes open. Maybe you'll recognize something that will help you remember."

Adam did as Ben suggested, but nothing looked familiar. His mind went to the images he'd experienced that morning in his sleep and he decided to mimic them. He rolled down his window, leaned his head against the doorframe and peered up into the sky. The breeze was warm and fresh against his face. He stared at the blue cloudless sky. Nothing. He closed his eyes and asked God to open his mind so he would recall something. A tingly, sweet, almost tangy fragrance filled his nostrils. It was the smell of fresh pines. He opened his eyes and saw a thick canopy of tall pine trees above his head. Just like he had in his dream that morning. His mind started grouping them together. Why, he didn't quite know. Almost as if it was a game he used to play.

The car slowed down and he lifted his head.

"We're here."

When Ben's car stopped off the side of the road, Adam got out and followed his uncle through a narrow grassy patch to where the forest began. Something made him bend down to touch the leafy soil beneath one of the trees.

"That's where they found you, leaning against the tree. Up there, between those trees, is where the car had crashed. You must have fallen out or something."

Adam fell silent. His hands glided over the dirt then up the tree's thick trunk.

"No, I didn't. Someone got me out of the car and carried me here."

"Probably the paramedics, yes."

"It wasn't the paramedics. It was before they came."

"Are you sure?"

"I remember it. I remember his smell. He smelled like toothpaste."

"As far as I recall there was no one at the scene when the paramedics arrived, Adam. Maybe your mind is confusing things."

Adam walked over to where the car had been found, then turned around to face Ben.

"I'm not confused, Uncle Ben. I remember it. Very clearly. Someone took me out of the car and set me down beside that tree. He waited here with me until the paramedics came. Then he left. I watched him walk up into the woods over there."

Ben fell silent as he watched Adam walk back toward him where he had been waiting beside his car. When their eyes met it was his uncle who spoke first.

"You don't think…?"

"I do. Who else?"

"He saved you from the car crash, waited between the trees until the paramedics arrived, then left. That's why he was in the picture, watching, keeping an eye on you, making sure you were taken care of. How did I miss that?"

"I think the bigger question is why did he feel the need to hide it?"

The drive back to Tampa had them each contemplating their recent discovery in silence. There was no point discussing anything. It was blatantly clear the stranger had been at the accident to save him and he'd been watching over him ever since. Who he was remained a mystery.

As they approached the edge of the city, Ben suddenly diverted.

"Where are we going?"

"I need to pop by the care home to see your aunt. I visit her every afternoon. It won't take long. She probably won't even recognize or remember you. She was already in a bad state at the time of the accident. Once we get back home we need to figure out what that block of wood is. Something tells me it holds all the answers."

CHAPTER SIXTEEN

Oakwood Care Home lay nestled between landscaped gardens that overlooked a small man-made lake. It was serene and beautifully decorated, feeling more like a luxury hotel than a facility for memory-impaired individuals.

The staff greeted Ben by name as they entered through the main door to where they stopped at the front desk to sign in.

"You brought some company today, Ben." It was more of a question than an observation.

"Indeed I did, yes, Gloria. This is Adam, my nephew. He's visiting from the East Coast. Is she in her room?"

"You just missed her. She's about to start her art class. We were wondering where you were. I don't think

I have ever known you to run late for your appointment." Again, another well-cloaked question.

"We got caught up with something. Sorry. Maybe we can steal her for just a few minutes before she goes in?"

Gloria chewed the back of her pen as she weighed up the request.

"You know we don't like to disrupt our residents' schedules, Ben, but since this is your first offense I suppose just this once won't hurt. I'll get Barry to find her for you. You two can go ahead and we'll have her join you in the coffee parlor in just a bit."

"Thanks, Gloria. It won't happen again."

As they walked through to the informal coffee lounge, Adam nervously turned back to observe Gloria's stern eyes that hadn't left them.

"Oh, don't mind her. She's not at the front desk for nothing. Gloria's been here almost as long as your aunt has. Around here you need to keep eyes on everyone. We don't want anyone wandering off and not finding their way back."

"Perhaps I should wait in the car."

"Oh, nonsense. Your aunt Agnes will be elated to see you."

"I thought you said she doesn't remember anything."

"She doesn't, at least nothing that makes any sense, but she loves meeting new people. She was quite the social butterfly in her day."

Adam didn't remember his aunt Agnes when she finally walked into the lounge accompanied by a young male nurse who he assumed had to be Barry. She was of average height and somewhat petite in frame. Her white-gray hair was neatly pinned up on top of her head and her face was beautifully made-up and finished off with a pale rose lipstick and matching rosy cheeks. She was groomed to perfection from top to toe, complete with a pearl necklace and matching earrings. Up close her royal blue floral dress accentuated her big blue eyes that exuded joy.

"There's my beautiful bride. Sorry, I'm a bit late today, but I thought you might like some extra company."

"Yes, yes, company." She smiled as her warm blue eyes stared into Adam's face.

"Agnes dear, this is Adam, Becca's boy. Remember him?"

Her eyes locked onto Adam's face, then suddenly her wide smile faded.

"So tragic. Just tragic."

"Yes, yes! You remember. They were killed in the accident. Adam is visiting me for a few days."

"So tragic. Just tragic," she repeated, tapping her pearls with a flat hand.

Adam didn't say anything. It was as if he'd just met a complete stranger. Feeling somewhat uncomfortable he just smiled back at her. And just as quickly as before, her sad expression turned into a big broad smile again while her big blue friendly eyes remained fixed on Adam's face.

"The oak is so strong, isn't it?" she said.

"Yes, dear, this is Oakwood. We've come to visit with you." Ben responded before he turned away to whisper into Adam's ear.

"She's a bit confused. She's been talking about the oak trees for years. Only problem is, there aren't any. It's the name of the place that confuses her."

He pulled out a chair at the small bistro table and helped her take her seat before he settled in next to her.

"He must go now. The oak is so strong, isn't it?"

Agnes repeated the words over and over, her tone becoming more distressed each time.

"I should go wait in the car, Uncle Ben. Perhaps I am upsetting her."

Ben, clearly also taken aback at her insisting that Adam should go, didn't argue, and handed him the car keys.

"Fine, fine, Agnes. Stay calm. The boy's going. Hush now. Go on then, Adam, I won't be long."

WHEN ADAM SETTLED INTO HIS BED THAT NIGHT HE WAS exhausted. Having had such an abrupt early start to the day in addition to the emotional roller coaster of information that had swept through his body and yet still had to make any sense, he was desperate to get some rest. But no matter how hard he tried he could not switch off his mind. It was well past midnight already and the house was quiet, except for his uncle's chorus of snoring rumbles that every so often ended with a whistle. Careful not to wake him he headed off to the kitchen in search of a glass of water, after which he settled onto the sofa in the sitting room. The wooden object still lay on the coffee table after he and Ben had stayed up till late in a futile attempt to unlock it. He sat there quietly in the dark staring at it on the table in front of him. Through the windows behind him, the moon cast a beam of light directly onto the flat wooden object as if it was a bright flashlight shining down from the heavens above. *Why did you leave me this block of wood, Dad?* His mind spoke to the unseen as if he would hear his father answer. Ben was right. That block of wood carried enough significance for his father to have deemed it necessary to personally deliver it in the middle of the night. And to a man he hadn't cared to speak to in years no less.

Adam traded the glass of water in his hand for the piece of wood and held it up above his face under the moonlight, turning it over to where the numbered corners stared back at him. A rustle in the plants outside the window behind him caught his attention. He lowered the wooden object and turned to look out into the street in front of the house, but saw nothing. Deciding it must be a neighborhood cat, he leaned over to pick up his water. To his left, he heard a noise coming from the patio door. He recognized it because he had opened that very door when he was desperate for air the day before. He stayed there in the dark, glued to the spot, his eyes aimed at the patio door. Listening. The clicking sound of the latch was unmistakable. Someone was attempting to break his way in. He fell to his knees on the floor and crouched down between the sofa and the coffee table. His eyes strained in the darkness but the harder he tried to focus his eyes the more it caused him to see dull patches of black. His heartbeat thumped loudly in his ears. From down the hallway, he could hear Ben's snoring. He was still fast asleep and clearly oblivious to the impending threat. Adam stayed hidden behind the table, his mind searching for a way out. If he acted now he could still make it past the door to the phone in the kitchen to call the police. But as he lifted his body off the floor to make a run for the phone it was already too late. The muted sounds of the door sliding on its tracks had his heart skip out of rhythm and he fell back down into his crouching position. Soon after, he heard shoes squeaking on the tiled floor as the intruder entered the home. Trapped on the floor behind the table in the sitting room with nowhere to go and not a single thing with which to fight the intruder off, he could do nothing else but pray. And as Adam shut his eyes tightly and prayed for protection, he clutched the piece of wood against his chest as if his life depended on it.

Somewhere in the dining room, the footsteps paused for what seemed like an eternity before they turned and squeaked down the hallway toward the bedrooms. There was no waiting. He had to get help fast. Before the burglar made it to Ben's room. If Adam were to have any chance of getting to the phone to call the police then this was it. He lifted his head and caught a glimpse of the intruder from behind. Dressed entirely in black and wearing a matching ski mask over his face, the faint moonlight glistened off the gun in his hand. With his heart now caught in his throat, moving like a cat walking through a puddle of water, Adam dashed across the floor and into the kitchen. Once there he stopped to listen. The squeaky shoes were still moving toward his bedroom. His eyes frantically searched the dark corners of the kitchen for the cordless phone that, for some unknown reason, wasn't in its cradle on the wall. Concluding that perhaps Ben had taken it to have in his room at night he aborted the search. His attention turned back to the burglar's whereabouts. It sounded like he had made it into his bedroom. *Thank you, Lord, for waking me up so I am not in my bed.* But his uncle still was. Caught up in a moment of terror, Adam focused his eyes toward the dark passage. With the wood still gripped tightly to his chest, his foot snagged the corner of one of the stools at the center island and it clanked loudly against another stool. Suddenly his heart was in his throat and his feet numb with fear, as he stood there frozen with dread. Surely the invader had heard it. He tried bolting for the door, hoping since there was no other way out he could perhaps lure the intruder out of the house and away from Ben. But before he knew it the intruder had made his way back down the dark passage and without warning surprised him from behind.

Adam fought his way to the door and briefly swung around to assess the invader's position. Just as the gun fired off a single bullet toward him.

CHAPTER SEVENTEEN

lsbeth's hands trembled as she lifted the vintage hatbox from the top shelf of her closet. She had spoiled herself with the purchase when she had just finished college and started working her first job at the local bank. She stared at the Air Force blue colored box where she gently placed it on the foot end of her bed. Her hand traced the gold Burdine's Fashion writing on the lid as she recalled how she had saved every penny until she could afford to buy the hat. She had never felt more proud in all her life. Now, staring down at the hatbox with its iconic gold trim, she felt as if she was going to get sick right there in the room. It was the first time since she arrived at The Lighthouse that she'd touched it. She had prayed about it all night, but not found a definitive answer. Her heart said to trust God for his protection, but her mind still interfered. Fear had reared its ugly head again and now, where she stood pondering her ways, it was consuming her. It's just in case, her mind justified it. Better safe than sorry, it continued. Finally, she found herself lifting the lid off the box before she carefully peeled away the corners of a daffodil yellow silk scarf until she found what she was looking for. She couldn't bring herself to pick it up just yet where it lay snug among the yellow silk. As if it was something pretty that carried boundless value. She would have never bought it back then if it weren't for his wicked ways with her. To her surprise, her hand was steady when she wrapped her fingers around the mother-of-pearl handle, which was the very reason she had chosen that particular one all those years ago. It had been the only way she thought she could veil its purpose. Now the pocket pistol in her hand repulsed her. It was heavier than she remembered, but then she knew why. At the time, her heart had been heavy with hatred, and her plan to kill Kyle in his sleep far outweighed the actual weight of the small pistol. She thought of dropping it back in the box but didn't. It was as if something else had taken over her mind, her body. She released the magazine into her hand, checking that it was full before she slipped it back into place. It's strictly for self-defense, Elsbeth Porter! she reminded herself, barely conscious of her actions as she carefully buried it underneath her silk scarf in the bottom of her purse.

When she closed the door behind her, her purse

wrapped tightly over her shoulder and firmly tucked in under her arm, Jim was outside her door waiting for her.

"Are you sure you're going to be okay going to town all by yourself, Beth? Perhaps we should ask one of the other women to go instead."

"Don't be silly. It's my turn to get the week's supplies. I'll be quick. Besides, there is a very good chance he'll have gone back home already. I'm sure word is out that the police are all over this case. He'd be a fool if he hung around here."

The words might have made sense and given Jim some peace of mind, but inside, she didn't believe a single word that came from her mouth. She was a ball of tangled nerves. Kyle wasn't one who easily gave up on anything, and no one knew that better than her. That trait is what had gotten him into the senate after all. But she was prepared. Armed not only with the concealed weapon in her purse, she also had her summer hat and sunglasses in the car.

"If you're not back within the hour I'm coming to find you. Understood?"

"Understood." She smiled at Jim in a final attempt to convince him that she was fine before she promptly left for town.

JOE'S FRUIT MARKET WASN'T AS BUSY AS SHE WOULD normally have it. She was almost two hours later than usual which had clearly made all the difference to missing the peak shopping time. It was a known fact that one had to be there early to get the best produce. But today it wasn't about getting the best peaches. Being late was intentional in the hopes that she wouldn't be recognized and thereby attract any attention to herself. By now everyone who knew her would have long gone already. In and out, she reminded herself when she lingered over the fresh oranges for too long. She was almost done and felt relieved. With her hat and oversized sunglasses on not even Joe recognized her. It would have been a disaster if he did. His loud voice carried a mile and it would have drawn unwanted attention to her. She dropped a dozen or so oranges into her basket and moved on to the tomatoes. He must have thought her to be some celebrity passing through town because he hardly gave her the time of day. Joe wasn't exactly one to be impressed by pretentiousness. She moved through the market and down her shopping list with stealth. Covering all her bases, she paid cash instead of on account and quickly headed back to her car where she dropped her shopping into the trunk. She didn't once look up.

She glanced at her watch. She had taken only thirty minutes so there was time left to make a quick stop at the drugstore. She contemplated whether she should risk it but she'd been having trouble sleeping and wanted to get something that would help. But going into the drugstore meant that she wouldn't be able to hide behind her hat and sunglasses. She paused to surveil the small shop opposite the road. It looked empty and her car was parked right across from it. She'd make it quick. When the coast was clear she dashed across the road and slipped into the small store, unable to hide her presence when the small bell chimed above her head. She ducked in behind one of the shelves and swiftly made her way over to the sleeping aids. In the distance she heard the doorbell chime again, a reminder to hurry up. So she did. She snatched a packet off the shelf and started making her way back down the aisle toward the till while she searched her purse for some change.

With her nose in her purse, she turned the corner and accidentally rammed into the back of another customer.

"Oh, so sorry," she immediately apologized. But the words lodged in her throat the instant the man turned around and she suddenly found herself pinned into submission by Kyle's debilitating eyes.

"Well look what we have here. If it isn't my pitiful estranged excuse for a wife. I knew it was just a matter of time before the gutter would wash you up somewhere."

Elsbeth couldn't speak, nor could she breathe. Her legs were bolted into place, her body paralyzed beneath his scornful eyes. Run, Beth, run! Her mind yelled at her, but she couldn't. No matter how hard she tried it was as if he had cast that ever-familiar spell on her.

"Aw now, has the cat run away with your tongue? Or do I still have you powerless and mesmerized by my irresistible good looks?" He ran one finger down the side of her neck and stopped where it hit the collar of her blouse.

He repulsed every fiber in her body. *Not by might nor by power, but by your Spirit, says the Lord Almighty!* The scripture from Zechariah echoed in her mind. And with a power she never knew she possessed, her palms flattened against his chest and she shoved him back against the shelves. The frantic look in his eyes told her she had surprised him. In all the time they were married she had never tried that before. His eyes instantly turned icy cold. At whip-speed his strong hand gripped her wrist so tight she felt as if she would faint on the spot, his steely face preceding the profane words she hadn't heard in a very long while.

At that moment, as if he was an angel sent from above, Jim's sturdy frame wedged in between them as he took Kyle by the scruff of the neck.

"Get your filthy hands off me, you imbecile. I will have you arrested and locked up for the rest of your miserable life!" Kyle squirmed.

But Kyle's threatening words bounced like blunt arrows off Jim whose voice carried a calm power Elsbeth had never heard.

"You lay one finger on her ever again and I'll have you—"

"What? You'll kill me? How pathetic!" Kyle scoffed. "You don't know who you're dealing with, my friend."

But Jim didn't play into his hands. Instead, with one effortless thrust, he deposited Kyle three feet away onto the floor and swiftly ushered Elsbeth out the door. When he had her out of harm's way and inside his truck he swung his vehicle around and sped off toward the mission.

Next to him, Elsbeth was sobbing uncontrollably. Partly because her body was riddled with fear, but mostly because she could not believe that Kyle Rudd still held his power over her.

"There now, it's okay, Beth. He's gone."

She reached for a tissue in her purse only to find the box of sleeping tablets in her hand.

"He's turned me into a thief too!"

"No, he hasn't. I will settle it when I come back for your car later. You're safe now. He has no power over you."

"But he has, Jim! I might as well have been back in Maryland. I was completely useless. If you hadn't come in when you did he would have probably killed me."

"No, he wouldn't have, Elsbeth. You were in the middle of a drugstore. Besides, I think you are underestimating yourself. You were just caught by surprise."

"Oh, you don't know him, Jim. He owns half the police force! He has killed before, more than once. And he had his dirty police puppets cover it up. His power and influence are far-reaching to every corner of the country. All this has done is anger him, fueled him even more! He will not stop until both Adam and I are dead. And the worst of it all is that he will get away with it too. They will never find enough proof to convict him with!"

"Well, I won't let him, okay! From now on you will stay at the mission. When we get back we're going to tell Danny and the rest of the team everything. We are all here for you, Beth. You are not alone in this, not this time. And sending Adam off to go visit with Ben was the best thing we could have ever done. He's out of harm's way and as long as he is there, he will be safe."

CHAPTER EIGHTEEN

The room reeled as Adam tried to lift his head. His left cheek was flush with the tile floor and his body felt as if it weighed several tons. His mouth tasted of blood. From beneath the weight of his torso, he was aware that both his arms were being pinned between his body and the floor. Intense pain shot through his chest when he tried to move one arm out from underneath him. He groaned, coughing up a ball of bloodied saliva. With one leg bent at the knee he wedged his foot against the nearby wall and pushed down as hard as he had strength left in his body. The first attempt failed, so he tried again. He squealed with pain that came from somewhere across his diaphragm when he rolled himself over onto his back. Gasping for air, he used his feet to slide his body into an upright position against the wall. A little bit of blood had accumulated in his mouth again and he let it run out onto his chin, then wiped it away on his shoulder. His mind recalled the events before he hit the floor. He remembered staring into the man's cold dark eyes seconds before he heard the gun go off. Then he felt the punch to his stomach that had flung his body down onto the floor. He must have gotten shot, he realized. He dropped his chin and inspected the area below his sternum where the pain was coming from, surprised to see there was no blood. With some feeling restored to his hands, he lifted his T-shirt away and turned his body toward the moonlight that was pushing through the nearby window. A large purple bruise shaped like a book lay across his diaphragm but there wasn't a bullet hole. His hands glided across his chest and bruised forearms in search of a wound, but he found none. As he thanked God for saving his life, his eyes closed and with his head back against the wall, he suddenly thought of Ben. The sobering thought had him react instantly and he peeled himself off the floor. At first glance, there was no sign of his uncle or the intruder. Deciding to be cautious in the event of the intruder still being inside, he slowly started down the passage toward his uncle's room, still holding his stomach.

The house was deathly quiet. As he passed the entrance to his own room he glanced back. In the faint dawn light, he caught sight of the bottom of his uncle's feet where he lay half-concealed behind the bed on the carpet.

"No, no, no!" he muttered underneath his breath while he rushed over to his side.

"Uncle Ben, can you hear me?" he called out in a loud whisper for fear of the burglar still being inside the house.

His uncle didn't answer.

Adam lowered his ear over Ben's mouth, groaning with pain again as he did so. His uncle was still breathing. His eyes searched for any wounds, relieved when he didn't find any. There was the beginning of a bruise on his jawbone so he patted Ben's cheeks to wake him up, increasing the intensity after the first few.

Ben moaned as he came to.

"You're alive? I thought he'd killed you," Ben mumbled.

"I did too. How about you?"

"The fool sucker-punched me across the jaw, but I'll live. Are you sure you're okay? I could've sworn I saw him shoot you."

"He did. He must have missed."

"Speaking of the devil, where is he?"

"I think you scared him away," Adam teased as he helped Ben to his feet.

"I'm going to do a quick check though, just to be safe."

Adam's brisk sweep turned up empty and he met up with his uncle where he stood assessing the scattered contents of his house in the living room.

"He's gone, Uncle Ben."

"Lucky for him! He turned my house upside down. What happened?"

"I have no idea. I couldn't sleep so I came in here to have another go at the box when he surprised me."

The piece of wood! Adam suddenly panicked. It was gone. His eyes skimmed over the sofa and through the items that lay scattered across the floor in front of them.

"Tell me he didn't take the block of wood," Ben said nervously.

"I had it right here on the sofa when he broke in through the door. Then I hid here behind the table."

Adam started searching through the items on the floor, frantically looking under and behind the sofa.

"Give it up, son. I now know why you are still alive." Ben's words came at him from across the sitting room where the intruder had shot Adam and left him by the front door.

Perplexed by his uncle's words, Adam joined him where he had bent down to pick something up from the floor.

"It's the slab of wood!" Adam yelled with excitement.

"Yup, except now it has a bullet lodged smack bang in the center of it. It seems this little piece of timber saved your life, Adam."

Adam traced his fingers over the bullet. The cold metal felt foreign to his touch. As his mind quickly worked its way through what might have happened, he lifted his shirt and held the wooden item up to the large bruise that perfectly matched its shape. He recalled having had the slab of wood clutched to his chest when he got shot and somehow, by the narrowest of margins, the bullet had missed both his arms and miraculously found its way into the wood. He smiled, in awe of God's hand. He had asked his Savior for protection and he had not failed him.

Ben's hand came to rest on his shoulder.

"If I hadn't seen it with my own eyes I would have never believed it."

"Oh ye, of little faith!" Adam smiled while quoting Jesus' words to his disciples during the storm.

"Yeah, yeah, you are right. I bow my head in conviction. I know it's really early in the morning, but how about a strong cup of coffee before we get stuck into solving that mysterious piece of wood once and for all. I have this niggling feeling that it's somehow linked to our unannounced visitor tonight."

"Shouldn't we call the police?"

"And say what?"

"The guy broke into your house and nearly killed me, Uncle Ben. I'm sure the neighbors can attest to hearing the gunshot."

"Oh, I doubt that, son. The guy was smarter than he looked." Ben was already in the kitchen preparing the coffee.

"I don't understand."

"The neighbors wouldn't have heard a thing, Adam. His weapon was equipped with a silencer. I saw it with my own eyes before he clouted me with the thing. Besides, with that bullet stuck in the wood, they'll be forced to confiscate it for forensic testing and such. It will get locked in an evidence locker somewhere and we can kiss any chance of finding out what it is goodbye. By the Lord's grace, we have both escaped this ordeal unscathed. Best we finish what we started and get to the bottom of this mysterious block of wood."

Adam couldn't disagree with Ben. His uncle's assessment was accurate.

"Do you think he broke in looking for it?"

"No way of knowing, but in light of all that has happened so far, I wouldn't brush it off as a coincidence. In all my years living in this house, I have never even had an attempted break-in, much less by a guy looking like a professional hitman. I reckon the fella came here looking for something specific, all right. He just didn't quite know what it looked like."

Ben popped a steaming hot cup of coffee in front of Adam where he now sat at the dining table. Adam had the slab of timber on its side, inspecting it from a distance.

"I don't believe it!" Adam shrieked without warning, nearly sending both cups of coffee off the table.

"What? You just about gave me a heart attack!"

168

"I can't believe it!"

"Yeah, you said that already."

"It's been right here in front of me this entire time! I can't believe I didn't get it sooner."

"Okay, don't mind me, genius. I'll just sit here quietly drinking my coffee until you decide to let me in on your revelation."

Adam was beside himself with excitement.

"Look! It's so obvious to me now. We've been looking at the numbers all wrong." He turned the slab upright and pushed it into Ben's full view before he explained.

"We had the block horizontal, assuming the shorter sides were supposed to be on either side with its longer sides facing us. Like this. The numbers run vertically down from each corner. Done purposefully if you ask me. Now, if we turn the wood on its side, the numbers run horizontally across, right?"

"Okay?"

"See these here? We just assumed they were odd markings in the wood. But they're not. They're longitudes and latitudes." Adam waited for his uncle to catch up.

"These are geographic coordinates."

"Exactly! Longitudes and latitudes. Together, in the right sequence, they mark a specific location."

"Well, what do you know? Your mother always said you were smart, Adam, but this? Do you realize how many years I have spent trying to solve this thing? I probably wasted half my life on these numbers."

"Well, they weren't supposed to be easy. It's a cryptogram. This was how they communicated with each other during the war. Not only are they written vertically and facing the wrong way, they're also written back to front. It's genius!"

"I'll get the map. I have it over there in the bookcase. Of course, it's probably now lying somewhere buried under a pile of books on the floor."

Ben rummaged through the items that had been thrown from his bookshelf.

"Found it!"

With the large map spread open on the dining table, they quickly moved through the numbers, circling the location with a red marker Ben had found in a nearby drawer. It didn't take them long once they knew what to look for but once they did, neither had quite expected the result.

"This has to be wrong," Ben remarked. "It's just not possible. Do it again."

Adam shared his uncle's disbelief and tracked the numbers again. But the result was the same.

"It's not an error, Uncle Ben."

"It has to be, Adam. Perhaps you scrambled it or misread a number or two. You know, this box is old and the etchings might have faded in places. You could have mistaken this for an eight when it's really a three."

Adam dropped the marker onto the table and stared at the red 'X' on the map in front of them.

"I didn't make a mistake, Uncle Ben. I checked every digit three times. I'm sure of it."

Ben didn't argue. He knew his nephew hadn't made any errors. He had checked the numbers himself.

Staring at the map, stunned beyond belief, the two men hovered in silence over the red, circled words that marked the precise location of The Lighthouse.

CHAPTER NINETEEN

The drive heading back to the East Coast seemed to drag on for an eternity. Adam had left within an hour of deciphering the cryptogram while Uncle Ben had decided Aunt Agnes was in dire need of some time away from the home. But Adam knew that was just an excuse. Ben had invested twenty years of his life trying to crack the mystery surrounding the wooden block and he wasn't about to give it up now. So it was agreed that he would collect Agnes first thing in the morning and take a plane to meet up with Adam in Turtle Cove.

It had been a rough couple of days and the painful bruise reminded Adam of that every time he had to move, cough or sneeze. But the prospect of finding out where his father's gift might lead was undeniably exhilarating.

He glanced at the piece of wood that lay on top of

his gym bag on the seat next to him. He smiled. Twenty years ago his father, for reasons still unknown to him, had left this object for him. Why, he didn't yet know, but he wouldn't rest until he found the answer. And in the back of his mind, a few more questions also lingered. Who killed his parents and why? Was it because of this piece of wood? Was there something locked between the layers of the wood? He was only twelve at the time and it had now become very clear to him that he had blocked the trauma from his mind. But spending time with Ben had stirred his memory and he found himself suddenly recalling several details from his childhood. He remembered his mother always being at home, and his father disappearing for weeks at a time. He recalled the school kids bullying him, calling him names. How his father and he would unscramble letters or numbers on the mustard yellow carpet in their sitting room and how proud he was when he had beaten him to it.

It was all coming back to him. But he still couldn't recall ever seeing the wooden block that seemed to have unleashed the unseen power of an enemy unknown to him. An enemy that he was convinced had killed his parents and left him orphaned. Straight away, conscious of the fact that he might very well have a target on his back, he took a quick look in his rearview mirror. No one was following him. In fact, there hadn't been a single car on the road in either direction for several miles now. Perhaps the intruder thought he had killed him. Perhaps the break-in was unrelated to his father's gift or the thief didn't find what he had hoped he would. Perhaps the enemy was just messing with his head.

He looked down at the speedometer and decided to pick up the pace. The sooner he got back to The Lighthouse the better, especially since Ben and Agnes would fly in that afternoon.

He glanced at the slab of dark brown wood again. He had the coordinates, which was great, but he had no idea where to even start his search once he was there. More importantly, what was he meant to be looking for that would unlock the secrets it held—and which he so desperately sought to understand.

While his mind tried to work through the enigma, he recalled the storage boxes Jim had left in Elsbeth's cabin when he had salvaged what was left after the fire. He had forgotten about them. Or perhaps avoided them.

Daniel and Elsbeth had given him and Ruth the cabin as a wedding gift. Apparently, it had belonged to his mother. He always thought it was just a tale they had spun to help him deal with the loss of his parents, but then Ben confirmed it with the pictures in the photo album. It was the very cabin they used to stay in during their childhood holidays at the mission.

A rush of excitement pushed through his insides. He'd start his search with whatever remnants were left of the cabin. It would probably be a wild goose chase since it had burned to the ground but at least it was a start.

About an hour away from the mission, still deep in thought with all he had learned and experienced during the trip, he realized it had been a while since he made sure he wasn't followed. The traffic had picked up and there were several cars behind him. He tried memorizing a few of them, reminding himself to keep an eye out, just in case.

When he turned off the freeway toward the bridge where he needed to cross the state park lake, he noticed that the black SUV that had trailed three cars behind his turned off too. A sudden bolt of energy hit him in the pit of his stomach, echoed by a distant voice that told him it wasn't a coincidence. He drew in a deep breath to rid his body from the fear, flinching when his bruise sent fresh ripples of pain through his middle. He shuffled into a more upright position and tightened his hands in the ten-two position on the steering wheel as if he sensed he needed to be ready. Deciding to put his premonition to the test, he increased his speed and glanced back at the vehicle. It sped up also. The action confirmed what his gut had already told him. Someone was following him. *How did I miss them?* It didn't matter. All that mattered was that he needed to get away from them. He turned in the hope of assessing the level of threat but the vehicle's tinted windows prevented him from seeing anyone.

He tried to stay calm, but in about another mile or so

he would be on the bridge where the road would change from two lanes to one and he wouldn't be able to go as fast. If they had any ill intentions the bridge would provide the ideal place to push him off and into the lake. Deciding that he should gain as much distance between them as he could, he pushed his car even faster. With his eyes fixed on the SUV behind him, he also noticed a second car trailing about a quarter of a mile behind. A silver sedan with normal windows. There was nothing ominous about it, which gave him some peace of mind. They'd at least bear witness or aid to any atrocity that might befall him.

Adam pushed his foot flat on the accelerator while he reached over to close the zip over the wooden gift in the bag next to him. He was ready. In the mirror, he saw them increasing speed too and he asked God to protect him once again. As if it was a film that played in slow motion, he watched the black SUV gain on him, yard by yard until it was on his tail. In the mirror, he could now make out the driver. A man appearing to be of average build wearing a white turtleneck under a black waistcoat with a dark-colored flat cap on his head. The passenger seat was empty. A charm dangled from his rearview mirror. Possibly a German flag, Adam wasn't sure.

The steering wheel shuddered under Adam's tight grip as he hit the inlay in the road that marked the start of the bridge, almost sending his vehicle out of control. A brief wave of panic washed over him and he found himself react by reciting Nahum 1:7 out loud as if he were shouting it at his follower to hear. *The Lord is good, a stronghold in the day of trouble!*

Against his better judgment, Adam's foot pushed harder on the accelerator until it was flush with the floor. But the black car was faster. Every cell in his body was on high alert as he watched the car close the final gap between them. A second later, Adam's body thrust forward toward the steering wheel as the man rammed into him, causing him to almost drive into the railing. Adam had felt that thrust before. When he was twelve.

When he regained control over his car he dropped a gear and tried to distance his vehicle from the man, but it only lasted a moment before another hard bump pushed against his car's rear. A feeling of dread crept up from the pit of his tight stomach. They were already halfway across the bridge that ran over the lake. Suddenly the terror of being pushed over the bridge and sinking to the bottom of the lake sucked the very breath from his lungs. No! You will not waver! he reprimanded himself.

In his side mirror, something caught his attention. It was another man, leaning out of his window. He had a gun in his hand. Every muscle in his body froze while his heart hammered faster against his chest. He moved the car over into the oncoming lane to avoid his aim and glanced back in the mirror. The man with the gun wasn't leaning from the black SUV. He was leaning from the silver sedan.

"Great! Now there's two of them after me!" Adam shouted out into space. And just as the SUV clipped his car's rear bumper again, a single bullet whistled through the air and shot into the SUV's back wheel. The impact yanked the vehicle sideways and thrust Adam's car across the road before it slammed against the railing. Adam felt his body pinned against his door as the car spun out of control before it came to an abrupt stop against the opposite barrier facing the direction he had come from. Barely aware of his surroundings, Adam searched for the black SUV but neither it nor its driver was anywhere to be seen. He turned his eyes on the silver sedan that stood stationary in the middle of the road, its nose facing him, the engine still running, with no one inside. To the left, there was a gaping hole in the bridge's barrier that marked where the SUV had left the road and plunged into the lake beneath.

Adam didn't move. Instead, he stared out toward the silver sedan, waiting. Whoever was driving that car had saved his life by shooting the wheel of the SUV and sending it over the bridge. If he wanted him dead he'd have shot him already.

Adam's fingers flipped the latch on his seatbelt before he yanked at the lever to open his door. It was stuck so he tried to open it by pushing his shoulder against it. His head hurt and he felt dizzy. He looked up to see the shooter step out from behind the trunk of his car and move toward him. Suddenly doubting whether he should get out of his car he stopped and waited to see what the shooter did next. A sharp pain suddenly stung behind his left eye and he reacted by pushing his palm down on his brow. It made it worse. Something trickled down and into his eye that left his vision blurry. It was blood. He tried to wipe his eyes but couldn't. His body felt heavy and he wanted to go to sleep. As he struggled to stay awake he was aware of a male voice speaking somewhere next to him. He recognized the voice. It was the same voice he had thought to be God bringing him back from his visit with Ruth and Abby. It was the voice belonging to the stranger.

CHAPTER TWENTY

When Adam came to, his eyes met with a concrete ceiling above his head. A strong smell of spearmint flooded his nostrils that made him wiggle his nose. The dull ache behind his left eye instantly reminded him of what had happened: he had crashed into the side of the bridge. He must have passed out and was somehow taken to a hospital.

The mint smell was suddenly right next to him and he turned his head to find the source.

"You're okay. You're safe." The stranger's voice, followed by a fresh wave of mint, suddenly spoke calmly next to him.

It startled Adam and he jolted into a seated position.

"You? Who are you? Where am I?"

"We'll get to that. All you need to know for now is that you're in a medical facility at our base."

"Base? Like a military base?"

The stranger nodded.

Adam studied the stranger's clothing. He wasn't wearing a uniform. He wore denim jeans and the same black trench coat he'd had on every time he had seen him. Adam swung his legs over the low steel cot. He was still dressed in his own clothing, so he couldn't have been in a hospital, at least not one that looked like this. The room was large with concrete walls that matched the floor and ceiling. In the far corner, a single gray steel desk and chair stood pushed against the wall next to a matching steel filing cabinet. Next to that, the entire wall was covered with photos and several maps, each with a multitude of red pins stuck in them. The room was poorly lit but three particular photos that were placed horizontally next to each other along the top of the wall had Adam out of bed and in front of the wall in just a few strides.

"Why do you have photos of me and my parents? What's all this?"

"Surveillance."

"I can see that. Why? What's it for?"

"Your safety."

"My safety, right, of course. And who might this guy be?" Adam paused in front of a photo further along the wall next to a map of Europe.

"That's the guy who has been on your tail for the last twenty years. That's an old photo."

It didn't take Adam long to recognize the man.

"He's the guy who tried to run me off the bridge."

The stranger nodded.

"He's also the man who broke into your uncle's house."

"He's the same guy?"

The stranger nodded.

"Did you kill him, on the bridge?"

"I'm not in the business of killing people." He popped a fresh mint in his mouth.

"But you shot at his vehicle and sent him to his death over the bridge."

"Affirmative. To protect you."

"So he's dead then."

"No. He's being held for interrogation."

"Why?"

"It's classified."

"Right. Why is he after me?"

"He was on assignment."

"Assignment, what type of assignment?"

"An assignment initiated by a hostile government."

"A hostile government. As in an enemy country. That's absurd. I don't have any enemies so I fail to understand how this involves me. I've never even left the United States."

"That might be, but unfortunately it has to do with your father."

"My father?"

"Do you always repeat every answer?"

"Only when it doesn't make sense. Do you always deflect with your statements?"

"You can ask me anything you wish. Most of which I will answer."

"Okay, so what does my father have to do with this? He's dead."

"And that was a very unfortunate incident. As one of our top agents, he was more involved than you might think."

"You have lost your mind, Mr.—"

"You can call me Gabriel."

"Gabriel, huh. Like the archangel," Adam scoffed, finding the entire conversation ridiculous.

"If you wish."

"Okay, enough with the cryptic sentences and vague answers, Gabriel. I don't know the first thing about you or what all of this is." He waved the back of his hand toward the wall. "But I do know that my father wasn't a secret agent of any kind. He couldn't have been."

"How would you know?"

"Because he was my father." Suddenly Adam recalled all Ben had told him and wondered if it might be true.

"You were twelve, Adam. You were just a kid. Your father was one of our best. If he couldn't fool his family, he wouldn't have been good at his job."

"And what job was that exactly?"

Gabriel didn't answer.

"Right, so I am on a *need to know basis only.*" His fingers made air quotes along with his sarcastic tone.

Gabriel didn't answer.

"Listen, for reasons still unknown to me you have had me and my family under surveillance for what looks like years. I think you're clearly making a mistake here. My parents died a very long time ago, and as I said, I lead a simple life and have never left the country."

"There's no mistake. You have something of great value in your possession. One that could jeopardize the safety of this country if it lands in the wrong hands. Something your father left in your care."

Gabriel's words drove an imaginary fist into Adam's stomach.

"My father is dead."

"Yes, he is."

"So you can see how absurd this sounds. He couldn't have given me anything."

Gabriel didn't comment, but the look in his eyes told Adam that he was very serious.

"Okay, enough already, Gabriel, or whoever you are. If this is your idea of some kind of twisted joke, it isn't funny. This is my life you are talking about. I demand that you tell me where I am and what it is that's going on here! Who are you and why have you been stalking me?"

Please, Lord, let me remain calm. Help me understand all of this.

There was a long silence in the room before Gabriel finally spoke again.

"Come with me."

There was no time to protest. Gabriel had already started punching in a series of numbers on a keypad against one of the walls which moments later had the concrete recede and slide to one side to open a doorway.

"Are you coming or not?" he called back at Adam who had remained frozen to the spot.

Adam followed Gabriel along a concrete corridor to where they soon stopped in front of another keypad that rolled away another door, and then Adam found himself inside a room three times the size of the one he had just woken up in. It looked much the same, except for about two dozen men and women dressed in military uniforms who either sat at desks or dashed between computers and several odd-looking sophisticated machines.

"What is this place?"

"This is Pegasus, our US military intelligence unit responsible for intercepting enemy liaison."

"Wait! They're codebreakers. Like the Ritchie Boys and Bletchley Park during World War II."

"Correct. Your father was one of our top codebreakers."

"My father, a top-secret military intelligence agent. You're joking, right?"

"I don't take my work lightly, Adam. He was one of our best. We intercepted a coded message and your father decrypted it. But the enemy tracked him down before he could get it to us and... It was unfortunate that you and your mother were in the vehicle with him. We didn't see it coming."

Adam couldn't speak. It was as if someone had squeezed all the air from his lungs. Nothing Gabriel said made any sense. At least not to him. Could it all be true? Could this stranger be telling the truth? Did his father live this secret life he had kept hidden from everyone he was supposed to love? His chest felt tight and no matter how hard he tried he couldn't get any air to his lungs. He tugged at his bloodstained collar that now sat tight around his neck, then turned to find a window or a way out. But found none. He spun around to exit through the door they had just used, but it had already shut firmly behind them.

"Let me out. Open the door, Gabriel!"

He did.

"How do I get out of this place? I want to leave. You hear me? They're expecting me at home," Adam said while he frantically searched for a way out of the building.

"This way."

.   .   .

WHEN ADAM FINALLY EXITED THE CONCRETE BUILDING, panting for air, desperate for clarity, Gabriel was right behind him.

"I know this is a lot to take in, Adam, but I can assure you it is all true. Your father died a hero, saving this country. He was a great man and a huge loss to the unit."

"What do you want from me? Why are you telling me this? I have lost everyone I have ever loved. My entire world came crashing down, and now you're telling me the person I thought was my father was in actual fact living a life of secrets and lies!"

"You're in danger, Adam. Now that they know you have the message they won't stop until they get it back."

"Okay see, now I know you're insane. I don't have any messages. In fact, I have no idea what you're talking about."

"You do. You might not know it, but you do."

Gabriel's words left Adam icy cold. He had the sinking feeling he knew the mysterious wooden gift his father had left him had everything to do with it.

"Your father was a highly intelligent man, Adam. He had prepared for this day, planned it to the finest detail."

"I don't understand any of this."

"You will very soon. But we're going to need to be very careful. Your life is in danger, Adam. Yours and everyone's close to you. They won't stop until they take back what we took from them. Your parents tried to escape them that day. But their plan backfired. And it cost them their lives. They were trapped. He couldn't jeopardize his mission or this unit so he did the next best thing. He hid it. He used encryption of his own and set it up so that, when the time came, and you survived the crash, you could complete his mission for him. He made arrangements to send you where no one could ever find you. The Lighthouse. It's what your parents both wanted and the only way they could protect you. Until now the opposition wasn't aware you had survived the accident. I was assigned to keep you safe for as long as it took. They've had your uncle under surveillance since the night your father visited him, before the accident. But the moment you arrived at his house it changed everything. They've been listening, watching, and now they know."

The information was overwhelming, but deep down it all made perfect sense. Adam took a deep breath and held it for several seconds before he spoke in a calm voice.

"What do you want from me?"

"We need you to retrieve the message. Find the message your father hid so we can neutralize it. This is your chance to finish what your father started. To complete the mission he sacrificed his and your mother's lives for."

"I don't have the message nor do I know where to find it."

"Your father said he prepared you for this and that you will know exactly what to do. He believed in you."

"Why is this message so important? It's been twenty years. Surely it wouldn't have any significance now."

"Unfortunately, it's exactly the opposite. If it gets out, it will cause irrevocable damage to this country and its allies."

"So it's some state secret or presidential sin."

"In a manner of speaking. The implications are huge. So huge it could start a world war."

"World War III. That's insane. People have been predicting a third war since the last one ended."

"That's what we do. We stop wars from happening. And this was no exception. If it wasn't for your father, the world as we know it would have been very different."

"What makes you think that I have this message?"

"Because they tried to kill you. And I think you know you have it. At least the first part. Your father must have found a way to pass it to you, and up until your visit with your uncle, no one knew about it. Now, you have a target on your back."

Adam could no longer deny it. Every fiber in his being knew beyond a shadow of a doubt that the gift his father had left him must somehow carry the message. Or lead to it.

"Who's to say you're not making all of this up?"

"No one. But I knew your father, and he trusted me

enough to have me assigned to you. From the day of the accident, when I took you from the car, to the other day in the creek. I've been right there all this time, watching over you. Your father left you a cryptic clue, which, once fully deciphered, will deliver the message. You have it, and we know you have already deciphered the first part of the cryptogram. It is my job to keep you safe while you break the rest."

"Why can't you do it?"

"Your father was a very intelligent man, Adam. He possessed a unique skill set that many of these code-breakers can only dream of."

"And what makes you think I know how to decipher this message?"

"Because the first one was the hardest and you have already broken it. Your father knew you would."

It was as if Adam's insides were in a chaotic jumble and he could no longer make any sense of his emotions. For twenty years he had been quite content not knowing the details surrounding his parents' deaths. It was an accident. An ordinary car accident. But here he was, suddenly tasked with carrying his father's secret legacy. And in the center of it all, buried underneath a thick cloak of deceit, was a mysterious gift his father had left him. One that lay dormant and buried. Fate rested upon his shoulders. A fate so huge that it would prevent a war.

"I don't have it anymore."

"We have secured your vehicle and its contents."

Gabriel's answer caught Adam by surprise.

"I don't know if I have what it takes to do this."

"Your father believed in you. You can do this. Also, we're running out of time. It won't be long before they realize their man is missing. We have less than twenty-four hours to find the message."

Adam turned away from Gabriel, his hands on his hips, needing to process what he had learned. And as Adam silently prayed for guidance, contemplating it all, he decided to listen to the faint whisper that echoed in his soul. The whisper that told him to follow his heart and to entrust his path to the one whose grace had helped him escape death more than once.

And as he took in his surroundings for the very first time, his Savior's peace descended on his soul.

Adam glanced at his watch. He was due back at the mission hours ago. By now, Ben and Agnes would have long since arrived.

"I'm going to need my bag back. And you have to take me home."

CHAPTER TWENTY-ONE

B en paced back and forth across the small parking area outside *The Lighthouse's* main entrance. It was almost eight p.m. and Adam hadn't arrived yet, nor had anyone heard from him.

"You're a bit on edge, Ben. It's not like you," Jim commented when he followed Ben out onto the front porch.

"Something's wrong, I know it."

"Nah, I'm sure he's fine. It's a long drive. Perhaps he stopped for a spot of lunch somewhere."

"Uh-uh, not today he wouldn't. And even if he did he still should have been back here by now."

His comment caught Jim's curiosity.

"Why not today?"

Ben realized he had said too much and tried to play it down.

"Oh, no reason. Just that we are here, you know, Agnes and me. It's been a while since she's visited the mission."

Noticing his obvious attempt at correcting his blunder had little to no effect on Jim, he quickly changed the topic.

"So what's with all the security all of a sudden?"

Jim decided not to push him, so he answered.

"Precautionary measures to keep the riff-raff out."

"Since when does Turtle Cove have riff-raff? It's the safest place on earth."

"Since the fire."

Jim's words left Ben cold.

"The fire. The one in Adam's house."

Jim nodded.

"Why? It was an accident, wasn't it?"

"I'm afraid not, Ben. It was arson."

"Someone deliberately torched the place and killed Ruth and Abigail! Why? Who would do such an evil thing?"

"We don't know yet. The police are still working the case. I have my suspicions though."

"You do? I'm assuming you told the police and they're looking for them."

"Not yet."

"Not yet! Jim, somebody murdered an innocent woman and her daughter for who knows what ungodly reason. Adam could have been killed too had it not been for him surfing. Wait! Does he know? Does Adam know, Jim?"

"We only just found out so no, we haven't told him yet."

"But you know who did it, yes?"

"Not exactly. We suspect it's someone from Elsbeth's past."

Jim had already said too much so he was cautious with his words. He didn't want to betray her trust.

"Elsbeth? How is *she* involved with these criminals?"

"She's not. It's someone who she knew a very long time ago and he's stirring up trouble, that's all. I have it under control, though. Hence all the security."

Ben came to stand directly in front of Jim. So much had happened over the past few days that made him wonder if the fire was meant to kill Adam too. Could the man who'd tried to kill him the day before have set it?

"Is Adam in danger, Jim?"

"Possibly, yes. But we don't know for certain."

But Ben knew, and the look in his eyes instantly gave him away.

"You know something, don't you, Ben? Tell me. Tell me what you know. Did Adam say anything to you?"

Ben didn't answer. Instead, he checked the time on his watch again and stared out toward the road that led up to the main gate. Adam was still nowhere in sight.

But Jim wasn't about to let it go this time. His instincts told him Ben was hiding something.

"Okay, listen, Ben. We've known each other for a very long time. We need to stop this and trust each other. Neither of us wants to see anything happen to Adam or Elsbeth or anyone else here at the mission, right? So what do you say we share what we know and put our heads together on this?"

Ben couldn't argue. Jim was right. This wasn't the time to keep secrets.

"Fine. I'll tell you what I know. We had a break-in at my house last night. The guy was a professional. He tried to kill Adam, but by God's grace, he missed. Quite miraculously too if you ask me. But the guy got away and I strongly suspect he might be after him to finish the job. I don't know for sure, of course, but I think I'm right."

He paused then continued.

"What if he is the one who started the fire? What if he had intended to kill Adam that day and didn't know about Ruth and Abby?"

Jim didn't know the answers. In his head, nothing made any sense. All he knew was that he'd promised Elsbeth he would make sure nothing ever happened to Adam. Not if he could help it. He turned and ran back into the building toward the rear exit.

"Come!" he shouted over his shoulder.

"Where are we going?" Ben asked as he followed him as fast as his bad knee allowed.

"We need to find Adam."

"How? He could be anywhere between Tampa and here."

"We'll trace back. There is only one road into Turtle Cove off the interstate. If we don't find him somewhere en route, we'll call the police."

"Sounds like a plan," Ben agreed, and they set off toward Jim's truck.

But as they came back down the garden path to where they needed to cross the lawns to the staff parking lot where Jim's truck was parked, Elsbeth came running toward them.

"There you are! I've been looking everywhere for you, Ben! You need to come quick. We can't seem to calm Agnes down. She's been circling the oak tree for a while now, mumbling to herself. She seems very upset, and we can't get her to settle down. It's getting worse."

Every cell in Ben's body wanted to cry *not now, Agnes!* But it was his wife, and he had dragged her all the way there and away from her home.

"She's probably confused. It's the name of that blessed care home she's in. I've been telling them for years it's confusing to residents. Who names a place Oakwood if there's not a single oak tree anywhere on site?"

As they set off toward Agnes, Elsbeth turned to them and asked.

"Where were you two going in such a hurry anyway?"

"Nowhere," both Jim and Ben answered at the same time.

"Okay, see, now I know the two of you are hiding something. I've been around these camp teenagers long enough to know when they're up to no good. Spit it out."

It was Jim who answered.

"We were going to find Adam. We think he might be stuck outside the gate. That fancy gadget is probably causing problems with the access code again."

He wasn't telling the whole truth, but it was all he could say to avoid Elsbeth going off in a panic.

Ben was quick to catch on.

"I'll see to Agnes, Jim. You go along and see if you can help Adam," Ben said to quash any further suspicions.

"Agreed. I'll catch up with you in a bit."

When Elsbeth and Ben reached the area of the garden where the tall oak tree stood, Agnes was a nervous wreck. Her usually perfectly coiffed hair was messy where her hands were pushing down onto her head. She was anxiously circling the tree while staring at the ground.

"The oak is so strong. Listen, it's talking to me," Agnes repeated over and over. Every few seconds she would stop and press her ear up against the tree, listening. Then she would start circling it again.

"There now, Agnes. It's just a tree. We're not at Oakwood now."

Ben tried to pacify her, to get her away from the tree. But she fought back, chanting the words over and over.

"No! I need to listen. He's telling me. I need to listen."

"It's just a tree, Agnes. It can't talk. You're just tired. Come, you should get some rest," Ben tried again.

But Agnes refused to move away from the tree.

"No, I need to listen. He's telling me. I need to listen."

Elsbeth and a few other women had gathered to one side, watching in horror.

"What happened, Elsbeth?" Ben asked.

"I have no idea. She was fine. We were just sitting here, enjoying the evening. And then she suddenly shot up and did that ear-pressing-against-the-tree thing. I told her it was just the wind rustling through the leaves, but she wouldn't hear it."

"What were you talking about before she got up? Something must have triggered her."

"Uh, I don't know. I can't remember."

"Think, Elsbeth, it's important."

Ben's eyes scared her.

"You're scaring me, Ben. We were just talking. I'm sorry. We didn't mean to upset her. She's been fine all afternoon."

Ben broke away from the group and went back to try and calm Agnes again. But she pushed him away.

"I'm not crazy, Ben," she said, almost sounding like the wife he once had.

When she said it again, looking self-assured and fully aware, Ben's heart leapt in his chest.

"Agnes? Is that you? Do you know who I am?"

"Of course I know you, silly. You're my Ben."

"Yes, yes, but do you know where we are?"

"You're acting silly." She laughed and now had her arms wrapped around the large tree trunk as if she was hugging it.

"Agnes, do you remember something? Where are we?"

"We're at the mission, of course. He had to, you know. He told me so."

"Who? What? Agnes, sweetheart, you're not making any sense."

"He had to. It's a secret."

And just as suddenly, his sweet Agnes whom he was certain was fully present again for the first time in many years, transformed back into the Agnes who had been trapped in time, blabbering non-sensical things.

"Maybe we should give her something. To calm her nerves," Elsbeth suggested. "I have something. I'll be right back," she said, remembering the drugs she had accidentally taken without paying on the day in the drugstore.

She dashed down the garden path toward her cabin and rushed through her front door, not noticing the door had stood slightly ajar. She didn't bother switching any lights on—she knew where she had left the box next to her bed. In the distance, she heard Agnes's rumblings and Ben's futile attempts to get her to calm down. So she hurried.

When she reached her bed and snatched the box off the bedside table, she heard her front door close behind her. It startled her a bit but it was a windy evening. As she turned to leave her bedroom, standing in the dark doorway, Kyle's eyes forced her to a dead halt.

CHAPTER TWENTY-TWO

J im's truck pushed along the quiet road toward the interstate. For some unknown reason, the digital lock was indeed jammed, so he'd reprogrammed it. He had waited for Adam outside the front gate but when, after twenty minutes he still hadn't arrived, he decided to follow through with his plan.

The road was quiet and he drove slowly so he could keep an eye out for Adam on both sides. Just in case he'd had a flat. He didn't want to entertain any other reason.

A helicopter flew overhead and he looked up to inspect it further. It wasn't the norm out in their neck of the woods, especially since he noticed it was a private one and sat lower in the air than one would expect. But he ignored it, furious at himself for allowing it to distract him from his task at hand.

When he reached the East Coast side of the bridge that crossed the state park lake, he felt anxious for the first time. So far he hadn't seen anything to indicate Adam might have run into any kind of car trouble, and there wasn't much road left until he would reach the interstate once he crossed the bridge. The thought entered his mind that he might have missed him when the aircraft distracted him. The notion left him irritated with himself all over again. He would cross the bridge and turn back once he reached the interstate if his search turned up empty. If he had missed him, he'd find him on the way back.

As he approached the middle of the bridge the moon sat low over the tranquil lake. Fall had set in good and proper already so the water would be freezing. If, by some awful act of evil, Adam had fallen asleep at the wheel and driven off the bridge, he would certainly freeze to death. The thought had his heart sink to his stomach and he begged God that his speculation was wrong. But when he got to the large gap in the bridge's barrier, his heart pounded frantically against his chest. He slammed on the brakes, nearly locking his wheels in the process, and took all of two seconds to rid himself of his safety belt and get out of his car. He had left his truck's headlights on full to see better. Pieces of broken glass lay scattered across both lanes, most of it orange and red from broken taillights. A large piece of wreckage lay a bit further up the road, so he ran to it as fast as his old legs would carry him. In the dim light, he noticed it was black—not white like Adam's car. *Thank you, Father!* He selfishly expressed his gratitude and quickly followed with repentance. He hurried back to the broken barrier, following the black paint marks along its way. It reassured him that the car that went over wasn't Adam's. He peered down into the lake. It was calm and he couldn't see any traces of a car. He'd call it in and have emergency services deal with it just in case someone was trapped down there. He got back into his truck and motored on toward the expressway, making a quick stop along the way at the roadside emergency phone. There was still no sign of Adam or his car.

As he turned back toward Turtle Cove he tried to convince himself that it was good that he couldn't find Adam. There was nothing to indicate he was in trouble. Adam could have easily decided to drive on past the mission and into town to grab an early dinner. It was possible. Highly unlikely, but possible. He passed the crash scene on the bridge where a rescue team had already arrived and was busy deploying the divers. He didn't have time to stop and check. It wasn't Adam. He had already decided he would head back to The Lighthouse in faith and hope that he had somehow missed him along the way and that he was safe.

ADAM JUMPED THE THREE FEET OUT OF THE HOVERING helicopter into the clearing between the trees. Gabriel had said it was the only way they would be able to go unnoticed. When his feet hit the loose dirt in the clearing, Gabriel lifted the helicopter back into the air and headed back to base. He had told Adam he would contact him the following day—his presence at The Lighthouse would be too risky and most likely compromise his mission.

The route from the forest along the beach and back to the mission was a familiar one. Just four months earlier Adam had walked it every day to visit Ruth and Abigail—and wait for the stranger. It all seemed so unreal. Like it was someone else's life he now recalled. Someone else's nightmare. His gym bag thumped against his hip where he had it crossways over his body as he headed toward the forest path that led down to the beach. When he passed the path through the forest to where Ruth and Abigail were laid to rest, he glanced back into the darkness at their headstones. It felt like forever since he'd visited them. He missed them. But he didn't have time to stop now, and when he reached the beach path, he yelled back into the darkness that he would come back to visit them as soon as he could. Right now, he had to finish what his father had started. The thought sat with him for a while as he ran along the beach toward the mission, gripping the bag where he felt the corner of his wooden gift push into his hip.

He hardly remembered what it was like to have a father.

His mind traveled to the piece of timber and the task at hand and he quickly checked the time on his watch. It was almost ten. Elsbeth might already be asleep. He'd have to wake her, he thought. Time was of the essence. The storage boxes with the remnants that Jim had salvaged from the fire were the only place he could think where to start.

The ocean roared noisily to his right. He also hadn't been in the water in a while. He missed that too and he silently vowed he would get back in when all of this was over. The sand was loose beneath his shoes, and by the time he reached the path between the dunes, he was out of breath. The small pedestrian gate in the perimeter fencing Jim had recently put up stood open. The padlock had been cut. It made him anxious.

He turned right toward the direction of Elsbeth's cabin. The Lighthouse seemed quiet. The air was crisp outside, so perhaps the younger members of the team were all up at the communal lounge. When his feet hit Elsbeth's porch her cabin was dark and quiet. He looked at his watch again. In the distance, he heard people talking. It sounded like it came from near the oak. Perhaps they had gathered around the firepit and she was there. He knocked lightly on her front door, just in the event she might be asleep. But no one answered. He'd let himself in, grab the boxes that he recalled stood just inside the front door, and go through them in his own cabin. That way he wouldn't disturb her, he thought. So he let himself in and quietly walked to where he'd last seen the storage boxes on the floor. Behind him, the wooden floor creaked. A second later the door closed. He swung around, expecting to see Elsbeth but instead found himself staring down the barrel of a gun. Holding it was a man he had never seen before. To his left, coming from Elsbeth's room, he heard her muffled moans, trying to warn him to get out, but he couldn't see her. It was too dark. His instincts told him to run to her, but the man's voice stopped him in his tracks.

"Now, now, don't you worry about her. You'll be joining her soon enough. Keep 'em hands where I can see them."

He emphasized his instruction by wagging his gun in an upward motion.

"Who are you? What do you want?" Adam braved.

"I don't believe you are in any position to ask the questions, son. Move!"

He signaled for Adam to join Elsbeth in her room, shoving the gun between his shoulder blades.

Elsbeth's muffled moans grew louder the closer he came to her. He focused his eyes in the darkness until he saw her sitting on one of her dining chairs in the middle of her bedroom. Her mouth was gagged, secured in place with duct tape. Her arms were tied behind her back and her feet tethered to the legs of the chair. At that moment Adam felt pure rage. Every cell in his body wanted to lash out at the gunman behind him, pull him flat to the ground. But he had the clarity of mind to know he couldn't possibly be faster than the bullet which would leave the gun that was pinned to his back.

In the far corner, a single candle cast a soft glow on the room. Elsbeth had been crying. That was clear. But what became clearer with each step he took closer to her was the bright red bruise to her cheekbone.

"You pig! What have you done to her? Let her go!"

The man let out a sadistic laugh.

"You have no idea who I am, now do you? Tsk, tsk, tsk. You didn't tell anyone, did you, Vicky?"

His words left Adam puzzled. Something that was very evident from his reaction.

"So, Vicky, are you going to tell him, or shall I?"

Elsbeth's eyes turned cold with anger, and Adam could see her jaw clench over the gag in her mouth.

"Oh, how silly of me. Of course, you can't tell him with your mouth taped shut. Your silence is so pleasing to my ears. I should have done that a long time ago."

He shoved Adam forward by pushing the gun deeper into his back until he fell onto the bed in front of her. With the moonlight streaming in through the thin curtains behind them, he could see the man's face for the first time.

"You're that senator. Rudd," Adam commented.

"Well look at you. You're a lot smarter than I

thought you'd be. But not smart enough. You see, this excuse for a woman here has been lying to you all along. Going around telling everyone her name is Elsbeth. Acting all religious like she's Mother Teresa or something. How pathetic! But you're just a fake, aren't you, *Vicky*? Just as pathetic as you were all those years you lived under my roof. You're nothing but a filthy—"

"That's enough! You have no right speaking to her like that, you hear me? Turn around and get out of here before—"

"Before what, little pastor? You make me? What a joke you both are. You know, you deserve each other. That wife and kid of yours were too good for you."

Adam's body went ice cold. Anger pushed through every vein and muscle in his body, shouting to lunge at this evil man who dared mention his beloved wife and daughter as if he knew them. But he couldn't because he had now cleverly pointed his gun at Elsbeth's head.

"I wouldn't do that if I were you, Pastor. Unless, of course, you want to see her killed."

Adam didn't react.

"Thought so. You're a coward, just like the rest of the pathetic losers of this world."

"Leave my wife and daughter out of this. They're none of your business."

"Oh, but they are. Or should I say *were*? I could have spared you a lot of heartache if my plan had gone as I had intended. But no. You had to be one of the lowlife beach bums around here and go surfing, didn't you?"

Confusion flooded Adam's mind as he tried to work through this man's wicked words.

Kyle sneered.

"I can watch you squirm all day, dear Adam, but I'm going to show you some grace."

"You know *nothing* about grace!"

"Oh, but I do. You see, I could have already killed little old Vicky here. Punished her for running away from me like that, embarrassing me with my constituents. But I didn't. I let her live much longer than she should have."

"Life isn't yours for the taking."

Kyle scoffed.

"That's where you are wrong. And your wife and daughter are proof of that."

CHAPTER TWENTY-THREE

A fresh wave of anger pushed up and lodged in Adam's chest as the implication behind Kyle's words dawned on him. It took every bit of strength not to let this evil man see the anger and unbearable pain he felt inside. He knew it was exactly the reaction Kyle had hoped to stir. *Lord, help me to stay strong. Help me to honor you in this.*

Kyle smiled a wicked smile to taunt Adam again.

"So you think you're above me, do you? Not quite the reaction I expected from you," Kyle said with a sadistic tone and then brushed the back of his hand against Elsbeth's bruised cheek.

"What do you want, Rudd? You have already shown us how formidable you are, so why don't you just go back to that hole you crawled out of and leave us alone."

Adam quoted a scene he'd once seen in a movie. It

was stupid, he was fully aware, but he was trying to remain calm—and distract Kyle from hurting Elsbeth again. But all it did was fuel Kyle's evil heart.

"What? You don't like me near Vicky? She's *my* wife you know. I can do with her as I please. She might have run away from me all those years ago but she never did have the courage to divorce me. So I still own her. Besides, I'll decide when I'm done here, not you."

"There's nothing here for you, Rudd. You won't get away with this. Let us go and you can still save that despicable political career of yours."

Kyle seemed unaffected by his idle threats, as arrogant, evil people usually are, and he turned the gun on Adam.

"Now that we've got our introductions out of the way, why don't you tell me why you're holding on so tightly to that bag of yours. And what's in those storage boxes over there, huh? Is that what you came here for?"

Adam's heart skipped several beats. In the heat of the moment, he hadn't realized he had clutched his bag to his chest. He couldn't let Rudd get his dirty paws on the box.

"Maybe you scared me and I needed to hold onto something," Adam said, hoping that his mocking would fuel Kyle's ego and he'd get distracted.

"Oh, you're a clever one, aren't you? Toss it over. Slowly."

Adam's bluff had failed. He tried once more by ignoring the demand.

"Really. You want to test me? Okay then, let's see how brave you really are."

Kyle pointed the gun away from Adam and pushed the barrel onto Elsbeth's temple. She shut her eyes and let out a faint whimper. Although she would die to save Adam if it came to that, she shot up a prayer for God to save them both.

"Ready?" Kyle asked while his eyes remained fixed on Adam's.

"One…two—"

"All right! You win. Take the bag."

Kyle smiled, conceit lying thick behind his eyes.

"Toss it over."

Adam slid it across the floor to Kyle's feet.

With his gun in one hand, still pointed at Elsbeth's head, he bent down and unzipped Adam's bag. One by one he pulled several items of clothing out before he suddenly paused and stared down into the bag.

"Well, well, well, what do we have here?"

Adam watched in horror as he lifted the wooden block from the bag and held it up to the moonlight.

"What's inside?"

"I don't know. Probably nothing. It's just an old keepsake."

"Old yes. Nothing important, not likely. Open it."

He tossed it back to Adam where he still sat on the bed.

"I can't."

"Oh yes, you can." He aimed the gun at Elsbeth's head again.

"No, I mean, I can't. I don't know how."

"Really? And why is that?"

From the curious look in Kyle's eyes, Adam knew he suspected it was valuable and Kyle wasn't about to back down. Then it dawned on him. He would use this opportunity to break the cryptography and hope for a chance to escape Rudd later.

"It's encrypted."

The declaration piqued Kyle's interest.

"Why? What's inside that it has to be encrypted?"

"I told you, I don't know."

"Well, I don't believe you. Where did you get it?"

"Believe what you want. I don't know what's inside and I don't know how to open it or if it's even meant to be opened."

He didn't. Not really, but he asked God to show him grace for getting so close to fibbing.

Kyle lowered the gun and crossed his arms, making sure it still pointed to Elsbeth.

"But you came here for something to help you open it, didn't you?"

Adam didn't answer.

"I'll take that as a yes. So what was it?" His eyes searched the room.

"I doubt this stupid excuse for a wife of mine will know anything, so what could you have come here looking for, huh?" The tone in his voice was almost playful, like he was a detective thinking out loud.

Adam purposefully looked away from where the storage boxes were near the front door. But Kyle was an intelligent man and caught on soon enough.

"Get up!"

He waved the gun at Adam's face and ushered him out of the bedroom. When they reached the middle of the sitting room, a few feet away from the cardboard boxes, there was a knock at the door.

"Elsbeth, it's me, Ben."

Caught off guard by the sudden interruption, Kyle yanked Adam back by the arm to face him. He raised one finger to his mouth while he aimed the gun to the spot between Adam's eyes. With mere inches between the gun's barrel and his head, Adam didn't dare make a noise even though he was desperate to. He couldn't risk getting Ben tangled up in this too.

"Elsbeth, I just came to tell you not to worry about getting something for Agnes. I managed to calm her down and get her to bed already, so I'm also turning in." Ben paused waiting for an answer from Elsbeth.

"Okay then, we're all off to bed, so see you in the morning."

They listened as Ben's footsteps turned and walked away.

When Kyle was certain he had left he spoke in his typical sneering tone.

"I couldn't have asked for better news if I tried. Seems no one will come looking for you two after all."

"Did you?"

Adam's question confused Kyle.

"Did I what?"

"Ask for help? You know, pray."

"You're a joke. I don't believe in God."

"You should. He can save you from yourself, you know."

"Oh, I doubt that. Look, he can't even save you, and you're supposedly his chosen."

"He will. When the time is right."

"Yeah? Before or after I kill you two pathetic losers? Now move it along. Bring those two cardboard boxes into the room and dump it out onto the bed. I don't have all night."

Adam did as he was told. He glanced at Elsbeth where she was forced into silence and looked utterly defeated.

"Why don't you let her go? I'll stay. Then you can kill me if you want. That's what you want, isn't it?"

"Oh, I want to kill you alright. But I want her to see me do it. I want to take from her what she stole from me and I want to see her suffer while I do it."

Elsbeth let out a pleading moan from beneath the gag.

"Did you honestly think I didn't know you were pregnant, Vicky? What kind of fool do you take me for, huh? Well, the joke's on you. If you hadn't tried to leave me that baby would have lived. But no. You thought you could run off to mommy dearest and take my child with you. It's your fault it died. You hear me? Your fault!" He shouted the words at her face, leaving Elsbeth broken and crying uncontrollably.

He had hit the very chord that had haunted her since the day she lost her baby.

"Leave her alone, Rudd!"

"Whatever! I can't wait to see her squirm when I kill you. But first, you're going to open that stupid little box of yours. I have a feeling that something important enough to be encrypted might just help me become the next president."

His admission left Adam ice cold with dread as he recalled what Gabriel had told him. If his father did, in fact, decode an enemy message that had prevented the world from another war, having it land in Kyle Rudd's dirty political hands would be detrimental.

"Well, don't just sit there. Get on with it."

"I can't see anything. I need the lights on."

"And risk being caught? Not going to happen. Use the candle."

Kyle pushed his chin out toward the candle that flickered next to the bed.

Adam did as he was told, and held the candle up over the bed. He had no idea what to look for, so he scanned his eyes over the items that lay scattered in front of him. He paused over one of Abby's favorite dolls, her hair scorched and half of her dress singed into its plastic body. He thought his heart would break in two.

"Stop playing with the dolly and hurry up! Your precious little girl doesn't need it anymore."

He had pleasure in taunting Adam, but God had given Adam the strength to withstand the enemy's vile attack. So he moved the doll aside and started working his way through the few of his home's contents that had survived the fire. There were only a few of Ruth's things, like her grandmother's pearl necklace, and a clay teapot she and Abby had painted together for Mother's Day. It tore Adam apart inside as he mourned their deaths all over again. His wounds were still raw and he felt as if he would collapse right there next to the doll. But Elsbeth's sudden gasps for air because the crying had blocked her nose, shocked him back to reality.

"She can't breathe, Rudd! Take the gag from her mouth!"

"Then stop your whining, woman. Got it? Don't you dare scream or make a sound or I'll kill him as slowly and painfully as I can."

She nodded frantically, breathing heavily the moment he ripped the tape and gag from her mouth.

"Happy? Now get cracking. You've been staring at the stuff too long."

"That's because I have no idea what I am looking for here."

Kyle walked over to the other side of the bed and pushed aside a few of the items on the bed.

"It doesn't surprise me. It's just a bunch of junk. I'll give you two more minutes, that's it. I'm sure I'll find a way to open it on my own."

He reached one hand into his blazer's pocket and pulled out a gadget he started attaching to the front of his gun. Adam assumed it was the same tool his uncle had said the intruder used on his gun to suppress the sound.

If Adam didn't find something that would buy them some time very soon, both he and Elsbeth would die at this evil man's hands. And as Elsbeth silently begged God to intervene, Adam allowed his hands to swiftly move through the remaining items on the bed. There was a photo, partially melted away but still sandwiched between thick panes of glass. It was a photo taken of him, Ruth, and Abby on the grass underneath the tall oak tree. It was on Abby's first birthday. For a moment he got lost in the picture as he recalled the day, losing track of time.

"Okay, that's it. You're playing me. I've just about

had enough of the two of you anyway. Say *adios* to your precious pastor, Vicky!"

And as Kyle Rudd prepared to finish what he had come there for, aiming his gun directly at Adam, he glanced back at Elsbeth to relish the look on her face and pulled the trigger.

CHAPTER TWENTY-FOUR

I t was almost midnight when Jim's truck came to a grinding stop at The Lighthouse. There was no sign of Adam or his car and it left an uneasy feeling in the pit of his stomach. He set off down the path and across the gardens to go look for him in his cabin, hoping he had made it back safely while he was gone. But when he reached Adam's cabin it was dark and quiet. Deciding he probably wouldn't be able to sleep if he didn't know for sure that he had made it back, he gently knocked on the door. Adam didn't answer. When he turned the handle the door was unlocked so he quietly slipped inside.

"Adam, are you home?" he whisper-shouted into the dark.

Again he tried but the answer was the same. Silence. So he walked down the short corridor to the bedroom and peered in through the darkness. The bed was empty and it hadn't been slept in. He decided to turn the light on in the hopes that he'd find Adam's bag in the room, but he didn't. Adam hadn't made it back home.

Jim wasn't a man that easily panicked, but right here, right now, it engulfed every cell in his body. He rushed back outside and decided he'd go wake Elsbeth, to check if perhaps she had heard from him. When he was just about at her door, in the crisp quiet of the night, he heard her tormented screams drift on the cool breeze toward him.

It was the type of scream he needed no explanation for. The kind that almost made his sturdy legs collapse beneath his body. And while he could have easily given in to its desire to have him drop in terror to the ground, his soul fought back. His aged legs leapt the last few yards up the path toward her cabin, and as he prepared to heave his body up the two steps and onto her porch, the far too familiar stench of fire smoke forced its way into his nostrils. With a strength he didn't know he possessed, he pushed himself onto the porch and made for the door. And as he reached to turn the handle, it flung open and his body collided with the one person he had hoped to never see again.

Kyle Rudd tried to push past him, but Jim was much stronger than he anticipated an old man would be. He threw the first punch and missed Jim's jaw by a mere inch or two. Jim had dealt with enough scoundrels in his lifetime and it didn't take him long to lift Kyle by the scruff of his neck and pin him against the wall.

"What have you done, Rudd? Where are Adam and Elsbeth?"

"You're too late, old man. They're dead!"

This time, it was Jim who pulled back his arm and punched Kyle squarely on the nose. The blow rendered him flat on his back inside the cabin.

"Jim! Help!" Elsbeth's panicked screams came toward him from between the flames in her bedroom.

"Elsbeth! I'm coming!" he yelled back.

But in that tiny moment, when Jim was distracted by the fire and Elsbeth's call for help, he had taken his eyes off Kyle. And as the flames emitted their bright orange glow, he saw Kyle pull a gun from inside his sport jacket. The dull click of the gun's trigger left Jim paralyzed to the spot as he waited for the bullet to pierce his chest.

And as Kyle Rudd had once again unleashed the evil that ruled his heart, in an act of supernatural, unfathomable, and divine power, the round lodged in the gun's chamber and the bullet failed to eject.

It took the length of a quick breath of smoke-filled air for Jim to realize the gun had misfired and he lunged down onto Kyle and flung a powerful fist across his jaw. Kyle fought back, pushing the gun toward Jim's head, but Jim's large frame overpowered him, and he forced another fist across Kyle's face. But Kyle wasn't one to concede defeat and he kneed Jim in the ribcage before he pushed him over and onto his back on the floor. Elsbeth's screams grew louder in the background and Jim fought back with every grain of strength he possessed, but it wasn't enough. Kyle's hand broke free from beneath Jim's grip and he prepared to take another shot. Out of nowhere, a walking stick thrashed the gun out of Kyle's hand before the stick landed against the back of his head and had him flop face down on top of Jim's chest.

"You okay?" Ben's deep voice yelled at Jim as he pulled Kyle's unconscious body off him.

"In there! Elsbeth's in there!" Jim waved for him to rush over to her as he caught his breath and stumbled to his feet.

"Ben! Help Adam! Get him out of here!" Elsbeth's panicked voice begged as she pushed her chin forward to draw his attention to where Adam was behind him.

Large orange flames raged next to Adam where he was lying on the floor beside the bed. He watched in horror as the scorching flames quickly worked their way through the linen and on top of the bed. Moments later Jim stumbled through the door.

"Get Elsbeth, I'll help Adam!" Ben yelled and pushed through the flames toward his nephew.

"Adam! You're okay! I've got you, son." He repeated the last few words more than once while he tried to assess his condition, spotting the large patch of blood on his leg. It took mere seconds for Ben to lift him into an upright position, his body tucked in under his arm to support him. Through the blaze, Adam saw Jim at Elsbeth's side and silently thanked God for sending help.

"The wood, where's the gift?" he mumbled to Ben.

"I'll come back for it, Adam. We need to get you out of here first."

And before Ben could argue, Adam had broken free and turned back to search for the wood slab on top of the bed. Between the roaring flames, he spotted it along with the last of his possessions, trapped in a fiery furnace, moments away from being engulfed by the flames. He had to save it.

"Adam, let it go! You're going to get killed!"

"I can't, Uncle Ben! It's all I have left! My father depended on me to finish his mission!"

The words left Ben confused and without the will to resist. Behind him, Jim's voice told him he had freed Elsbeth from the chair and was urging them to get out of there. And as Jim carried Elsbeth outside, Ben pushed Adam to one side and drove his walking stick through the flames that near consumed the bed. Though the flaming hot fire stung at his hand and face, he jabbed the wooden object with the stick and flung it off the bed where it landed on the floor near the door. With the encrypted wooden gift secured in one hand and Adam supported over his body with the other, Ben carried them to safety.

IT WAS DEEP INTO THE NIGHT, UNDER A STARRY AUTUMN sky when Chief Perry gave the all-clear and called his company to stand down. The paramedics had already tended to Adam's leg, which unbelievably turned out to be nothing more than a bullet graze that required a few stitches.

"You were extremely fortunate, Adam," said Chief Perry. "A few inches to the left and that bullet would have hit your femoral artery. You would have bled out in minutes."

"So I've heard. By grace I have been saved, my friend," Adam replied, his heart filled with gratitude and praise.

"Things could have gone horribly wrong here tonight. In all my years as fire chief, I have never had two cases of arson so close together, much less at the same location."

"I wish I could say otherwise but this time it was all my doing. I had to use the candle to impede Rudd's attack. It was a decoy in the hopes of escaping. Foolish, I know, but all I could come up with in the heat of the moment. No pun intended! Speaking of which, where is he?"

"Off to jail where he will spend a fair amount of time, my friend. It turns out he is quite the crooked politician. And he apparently has a thing for fires. Rumor has it he'd been accused of insurance fraud with one of his buildings some time ago. They just never had enough evidence to convict him. I reckon he needed the money for one of his campaigns. But the police chief tells me he won't easily escape conviction this time. They have enough proof to make it stick. And with Elsbeth's testimony, he is likely to go down on a lot more than just arson and insurance fraud. Speaking of which, I need to check in with him quickly. I'll catch you later," he shouted over his shoulder as he left.

Ben hobbled over and joined Adam.

"Well that was quite the ordeal, wasn't it? Glad you're okay, son. If it hadn't been for your aunt Agnes' flare-up in the middle of the night, I would have never come looking for Elsbeth."

"You and Jim saved our lives, Uncle Ben. Thank you. I should have never dragged you into this. I'm really sorry. And I'm sorry it cost you your favorite walking stick too."

"That, I can replace. You and Elsbeth, not so much. I firmly believe God's hand was all over this, Adam. As the scripture goes, *all things work together for good to those who love God.* Now, do you mind repeating what I *think* I heard you say in there?"

"It's a long story, but I met this man, Gabriel. He

works for the military. That's where I was yesterday. He saved me from the guy who broke into your house. Turns out the intruder is a hostile spy who was also the one responsible for killing my parents."

"Your father! Why?"

"You didn't know?"

"What?"

"My father was a codebreaker, a secret agent for the US military, and he decrypted a cryptogram that was intercepted beyond enemy lines. They found out and hunted him down to neutralize it, and him. The car accident wasn't an accident. It was an attack. To kill him."

"One that left your mother dead, and almost killed you too! And now you're telling me your father was a secret spy?"

"Exactly. He was killed in the line of duty, to protect our country."

"And this block of wood contains this cryptogram."

"No, it doesn't. It's a red herring."

"You've lost me."

"It was an instruction for me. Cleverly disguised in one of my father's codes. One he taught me to read when I was very young. It was a game we used to play on Sundays after church. For fun. At least that's what I thought we were doing. Turns out they were code-breaking lessons and I didn't even know it."

"So he left you a block of wood to lead you here, to The Lighthouse."

"Apparently so, yes. The very place he' and my mother made sure I'd end up in the event they both died. It was the only place no one would find me. That's why my mother had the papers drawn up and I was sent to live here and not with you. To protect me, and you."

"Makes sense. But what's this business of you needing to complete your father's mission?"

"I believe he hid the enemy message here, at The Lighthouse, and now they've tasked me to find it."

"Great! So we're right back where we started then."

"Oh ye of little faith," Adam teased. "I think I know exactly where the message is. And Aunt Agnes knew all along."

CHAPTER TWENTY-FIVE

I t was warm and sunny that afternoon when they all
gathered under the majestic oak tree where it stood
tall and proud in the gardens of The Lighthouse. The
afternoon autumn sun pushed through the golden leaves,
radiating beams of light down onto the green grass
below. There was a certain calm in the air that hovered
over the mission. As if a heavy cloud had been lifted
away. Even the large oak tree that had been there long
before The Lighthouse existed had a certain air about it,
its leaves glistening like pure gold.

Agnes beamed where she stood tall next to Ben. She
too seemed different. Though her mind was trapped in a
perpetual loop that no longer made sense to those
around her, she seemed calm and happy. Almost
expectant.

Gabriel had arrived an hour before, trailed by three armed military units that had the task of guarding the grounds. A sight likened to no other ever seen on the island before.

It was Ben who spoke first.

"What do you all say we unwrap this hefty gift my brother-in-law left behind? We've been waiting under this tree all day and I'm not getting any younger. Adam, it's time to be a hero. Show us what you got, son, and tell us why you had us all gather here. All these guns and soldiers are making me nervous."

Adam smiled.

"Let's not get ahead of ourselves here, Uncle Ben. I am not the hero. My father was."

He paused and looked at Gabriel.

"Ready?"

Gabriel nodded.

With his heart beating excitedly in his chest, Adam moved to where he had once sat on top of a large exposed root, next to Ruth with their precious one-year-old Abigail on his lap. Exactly as in the photo that had miraculously survived both fires. He stood facing the tree, one foot on either side of the large surface root that bulged out from beneath the ground. He ran his hands upward along the smooth trunk until his fingers settled on the marking. The very marking he now recognized to mimic one on the block of wood his father had left him.

It was barely there. Noticeable only if you knew what to look for. His eyes followed the three words etched at the bottom of the block of wood. Initially, he had thought it to be a manufacturer's seal. Like the 'Made in China' seals so often seen. But it wasn't. He now knew exactly what it was. He worked quickly; replacing each of the letters with a number of the alphabet, running the exact cryptogram sequence he recalled doing with his father when he was just a child. It didn't take him long and before he knew it, he found the next instruction. From the marking on the tree, he followed it, carefully tracing the measuring tape as prescribed. Three inches to the right, then up five, then ten to the left. Until his eyes settled on it. There, hidden deep between the thick folds of the large oak tree, the outlines of an object similar to a test tube and identical in color to the bark, lay safely buried in the layers of the trunk.

After he managed to gently retrieve it from the tree he turned and held it out to Gabriel.

"I believe you'll find the message inside."

And so he did. A small scroll written in his father's hand revealing the secret text he'd died to protect.

When all was said and done, and Gabriel left, they stood in awe of God's greatness. For although there was suffering, there was purpose.

The events of the night before had taken their toll on the entire team, but mostly on Elsbeth. She had cried all night. Not out of sorrow for all she had lost. Not out of shame for being exposed. Not out of joy that Kyle had at long last been brought to justice. But because she had finally truly experienced the gifts of grace and forgiveness; grace her Savior had shown her for the way she chose to leave her husband, grace for living a lie, grace until she managed to fully forgive Kyle and grace until she could forgive herself.

She had found peace. A peace so great it invigorated her entire body. A peace that could accept what had happened to her. A peace that gave her a new life. And although she was too old to ever have the joy of carrying a child again, God had gifted her Adam. To love and care for as if he were her own.

Elsbeth watched and listened to Adam as he shared all he had learned about his father, and the journey that had brought him there. For accepting the suffering he didn't deserve and knowing that it had refined him into pure gold. She recognized in him the same gift of peace that had led him to a place of restoration and forgiveness in the midst of another's sin in a fallen world. A peace so pure that it could only truly be understood knowing that through it all, God's grace was sufficient for them.

From the fullness of His grace we have all received one
blessing after another.
John 1:16

If you enjoyed this book/series, **please consider leaving a review.**

Thank you for reading!

BOOK 2 - When Carrie Claiborne mysteriously vanishes, Adam has to rely on his decoding skills to find her. But things get complicated when her estranged brother rolls into town. And danger is his companion!

EVERY GOOD PLAN

(Book 2 in this series)

CHAPTER ONE

For the first time in his life he felt fear. True fear. The kind of fear that drains your body of every other emotion and then spits you out to rot. The kind that penetrates the deepest, darkest corners of your soul and has you suddenly question the purpose of life. A life he didn't know was even worth fighting for. It would have been so easy to give up. He no longer felt pain. He no longer felt anything. This was it. This was how he was going to die. Death suddenly felt far more exciting than ever before. Almost welcoming.

As another fist slammed into his already pummeled

jaw he snickered inwardly. He had found himself in many tricky situations over the forty-four years of his miserable life, but this one took the cake. This time he had somehow gotten himself caught in a snare he didn't know how to escape from. And unlike all the other times he had come close to situations like these, he had always managed to talk himself out of it. Not this time though. This time his greed had finally caught up with him.

Perhaps his little sister was right all along. He was a good-for-nothing idiot who'd had this day coming. She'd certainly predicted it plenty of times. But she was too young to understand why he had chosen the life he had. It wasn't as if he ever really had a choice in the matter anyway. He had his father to thank for that. Now there was no turning back. His luck had finally run out. Luck. As if that really existed. His life had never been one filled with good fortune or success. He took whatever scraps had come his way and did what any other cursed sod would have done; survived.

Another blow to his nose interrupted his wretched thoughts. It yielded him nearly unconscious on the ground. His body pushed down hard onto his already broken arm. That was the first bout of punishment they had served him. But he had felt that type of abuse many times before. An experience that had made it easier. A bolt of pain shot up his broken limb as if to emphasize the memories he had worked so hard to forget. He wasn't numb after all.

In the distance he heard the command come to finish him off and suddenly he was faced with a decision. Should he give up or should he fight to live? But before he could answer his question the decision was made for him and he felt the sharp edge of a knife slam into his back. He counted four more thrusts before Lucky Lenny blacked out.

IT WAS DEEP INTO THE NIGHT WHEN THE SHRILL SOUND of a passing car's horn brought him back to consciousness. The sound of several more cars rushed past him, their headlights blinding what little vision he had left. As his mind tried to piece things together, he realized he was still lying with his face in the dirt, his broken arm pinned beneath his mutilated body. He drew in a few shallow breaths. His ribs made a cracking sound in his ears. Again a feeling of self-satisfaction came over him. It seemed neither he nor his attackers had any say in whether or not he should live. Something or someone else had had the final say. They had certainly given it their best shot at killing him. Left him for dead somewhere in a ditch on the side of the road. But they had failed. He had survived… again. But somehow his survival was different this time. He could sense it. Instinctively he knew that Lady Luck had nothing to do with it either. Then who did? Who decided he should live?

He managed to lift his head enough to see he was only about twenty yards away from the road. A road he didn't recognize. They had pulled a hood over his head before they threw him in the trunk of the car but if he had the chance, he'd wager on being at least an hour outside Atlanta. Another set of headlights pierced his retinas. Obscured by the shadows of a nearby tree and the pitch darkness of the night, he would likely not be noticed at all. If he could somehow crawl to the edge of the road, he would at least have a chance of being spotted by a passing vehicle. It was worth a shot. It was his only shot. The only one he had right now, considering his unfortunate predicament. He tried moving his right leg up to push his body through the dirt but couldn't. It didn't respond at all. They must have damaged the nerves in his back when they stabbed him. Instinctively he tried moving his left foot and felt the sweet sensation of pain from the sharp gravel under his bare toes. Relieved to have feeling in his left leg he pulled his knee in a forty-five-degree angle next to his weakened body. With his right arm broken and still pinned beneath his frame, he stretched out his left arm, digging his fingers into the gritty soil. He drew in another few short breaths before he pushed the side of his big toe down into the ground and tucked his fingernails firmly into the top layer of the hard soil. The push-pull action dragged his scrawny body across the damp earth—one inch at a time. Caught in the motion his broken arm was pulled along beneath his weight and he groaned with pain. When he finally caught his breath again, he turned his eyes in the direction of the road where another car just flew by. Again his left leg curled up into position followed by his outstretched arm. With his eyes pinned on the prize he drew in a shallow breath and pushed his body forward again. The familiar agony flooded his body once more. Except, this time he didn't flinch. He had shut his mind off to receiving it and kept his eyes firmly on the road ahead. Just like he had done all those times he was the receiver of his father's wrath. It instantly surprised him that he suddenly had an over-whelming will to survive. To live. Why, he didn't quite know. But he wasn't about to give up without a fight.

The short distance to the road would have taken less than a minute had he been able to walk it. Instead he had only gained a few inches at a time. There was no way of telling how many hours it had taken him to haul his near-lifeless body across the uneven dirt. But what he did know was that the time between passing vehicles had increased. As the cars became fewer, it was clear that his hope of being rescued was slowly slipping away with each passing second. Until the cars eventually stopped altogether.

The night grew eerily quiet. His body no longer felt the icy winter air that pushed through the thin fabric of his tee shirt. Somehow his body had adapted to the near-freezing temperature. Or perhaps he was already dead.

He forced his heavy eyelids open. Inches away from his nose his left hand stared back at him. Dark red patches of dried blood mixed with dirt lay in a thick crust around each finger. On two of his fingers his nails had chafed away to expose his flesh; evidence of how hard he had already fought to stay alive. Lucky Lenny refused to believe his luck had run out. He'd wait. For however long it took to be found. All he needed to do was stay awake. Stay alive.

WHILE HIS BODY NOW LAY HALFWAY OVER THE RIDGE where the dirt met the tarmac, sprawled like the crime scene sketches on his favorite detective show, he started to question the purpose of life. His life, to be more exact. Had he squandered valuable opportunities that had already come his way? Was spinning the wheel of fortune all his life amounted to? Who decided that for him anyway? His alcoholic father who'd beat him to a pulp just for the fun of it. Or his weak mother who'd finally had the nerve to defend herself. It's not as if he had planned to be born into this empty world that had never once dealt him a decent hand. But there he was. Born to be someone's punching bag. A tool that qualified his pathetic father to claim his drinking money through state grants. No, Lucky Lenny was everything but lucky. Every opportunity that had ever come his way he had meticulously planned. He had always created his own plans. Big plans. The last of which was meant to be the final payoff that would've set him up for the rest of his life. A chance to get away from his cursed existence. Yet, with all the odds stacked in his favor, his plan had failed. Or had it? Lenny paused to mull over his thoughts. Even if he did somehow survive this horrible twist of his fate, could he go back to a life that relied solely on luck? Did he want to?

And as he once again pondered the meaning of his shabby life, with his ear flush against the near-frosted tarmac, the faintest of vibrations drove into his eardrum. At first, he thought he was imagining it. But then it grew louder and louder. Until the wheels of a car screeched to a standstill right beside his head. Suddenly fear reared its ugly head. What if they had come back to make sure he was dead? What if they, in the interim, had discovered he knew more than he had let on?

But as quickly as panic tried to take over his broken body, something else, something far more powerful than fear, overwhelmed his senses. For the first time, he experienced hope. Not the superficial hope he felt each time he rolled the dice. True hope. The kind of hope that told him he had a chance to do things differently. A chance to do things right. A chance that had nothing to do with luck, and everything to do with survival.

The male voice next to his ear was calm and reassuring. Nothing more than a faint whisper. What Lenny imagined an angel would sound like. Not that he believed in heavenly beings of any kind. But he believed it when this voice told him he would live and that everything was going to be just fine.

CONTINUE READING

https://amzn.to/3mmz7Hm

GET YOUR FREE SUSPENSE THRILLER!

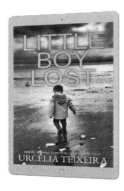

A MISSING BOY. A TOWN BURIED IN SECRETS.
A DEPUTY WHO WON'T QUIT.

https://home.urcelia.com

ADAM CROSS SERIES- CHRISTIAN
MYSTERY & SUSPENSE

Gripping faith-filled mystery and suspense novels laced with
danger and adventure that

will leave you breathless on every page!

Best enjoyed in sequence

EVERY GOOD GIFT - Book 1

EVERY GOOD PLAN - Book 2

EVERY GOOD WORK - Book 3

VALLEY OF DEATH SUSPENSE THRILLERS

Toe-curling suspense thriller trilogy you won't want to put down once you start!

Readers say this is my best work yet!

Best enjoyed in sequence

VENGEANCE IS MINE - Book 1

SHADOW OF FEAR - Book 2

WAGES OF SIN - Book 3

Fast-paced, clean archaeological adventure thrillers with a Christian worldview.

Inspired by actual historical events and artifacts

Also suited as standalone novels

Download the Free series prequel - download. urcelia.com

The PAPUA INCIDENT - Prequel *(not sold in stores) Free when you sign up*

The RHAPTA KEY

The GILDED TREASON

The ALPHA STRAIN

The DAUPHIN DECEPTION

The BARI BONES

The CAIAPHAS CODE

For more on the author and her books, please visit www.urcelia.com

MESSAGE FROM THE AUTHOR

All glory be to the Lord, my God who breathed every word through me onto these pages.

I have put my words in your mouth and covered you with the shadow of My hand
Isaiah 51:16

It is my sincere prayer that you not only enjoyed the story, but drew courage, inspiration, and hope from it, just as I did while writing it. Thank you sincerely, for reading *Every Good Gift*.

If you would like others to also be encouraged by this story, you can help them discover my book by leaving a review.
CLICK HERE

Writing without distractions is a never-ending challenge. With a house full of boys, there's never a dull moment (or a quiet one!)

So I close myself off and shut the world out by popping in my earphones.

Here's what I listened to while I wrote *Every Good Gift*:

- 10 Hours/God's Heart Instrumental Worship —Soaking in His presence (https:// youtu.be/Yltj6VKX7kU)
- 2 Hours Non-Stop Worship Songs— Daughter of Zion (https:// youtu.be/DKwcFiNe7xw)

When I finished writing the last sentence of the book!
How great is our God—Chris Tomlin
(https://youtu.be/KBD18rsVJHk)

AUTHOR CONNECT

STAY CONNECTED

Sign Up for Urcelia Teixeira's newsletter and get future new release updates, cover reveals, and exclusive sneak peeks and VIP reader discounts! (signup. urcelia.com)

FOLLOW ME

BookBub has a New Release Alert. Not only can you check out the latest deals, but you can also get an email when I release my next book, and see what I read and recommend. Follow me here
https://www.bookbub.com/authors/urcelia-teixeira

Website:

https://www.urcelia.com

Facebook:

https://www.facebook.com/urceliabooks

Twitter:

https//www.twitter.com/UrceliaTeixeira

ABOUT THE AUTHOR

Urcelia Teixeira writes gripping Christian mystery, thriller and suspense novels that will have you on the edge of your seat! Firm in her Christian faith, all her books are free from profanity and unnecessary sexually suggestive scenes.

She made her writing debut in December 2017, kicking off her newly discovered author journey with her fast-paced archaeological adventure thriller novels that readers have described as 'Indiana Jones meets Lara Croft with a twist of Bourne.'

But, five novels in, and nearly eighteen months later, she had a spiritual awakening, and she wrote the sixth and final book in her Alex Hunt Adventure Thriller series. She now fondly refers to The Caiaphas Code as her redemption book, her statement of faith.

And although this series has reached multiple Amazon Bestseller lists, she took the bold step of following her true calling and switched to writing what naturally flows from her heart and soul: Christian Suspense.

A committed Christian for nearly twenty years, she now lives by the following mantra:

"I used to be just a writer. Now, I am a writer with a purpose!"

For more on her and her books, please browse her website, www.urcelia.com or email her on books@urcelia.com

Never miss a new release!

Sign up to her Newsletter: signup.urcelia.com

Follow her on BookBub (https://www.bookbub.com/authors/urcelia-teixeira)

facebook.com/urceliabooks

twitter.com/UrceliaTeixeira

bookbub.com/authors/urcelia-teixeira

Made in the USA
Middletown, DE
01 September 2022

72878408R00158